T0019834

About the Author

Anthony Ferner started writing fiction back in the 1990s and has been a member of the Tindal Street Fiction Group since 2010. He has previously published three short novels: *Winegarden* in 2015, *Inside the Bone Box* in 2018 and *Life in Translation* in 2019.

With a degree in Politics, Philosophy and Economics from the University of Oxford, and a doctorate in Sociology from the University of Sussex, Anthony had a career in academic research. He was a professor of international business until his retirement in 2014, and has published numerous research articles and monographs on the behaviour of multinational companies.

Anthony is married, with two sons. He lives in the Midlands. His interests include Spanish and Latin American literature, languages and skating.

Small Wars in Madrid

ANTHONY FERNER

Fairlight Books

First published by Fairlight Books 2024

Fairlight Books
Summertown Pavilion, 18–24 Middle Way, Oxford, OX2 7LG

Copyright © Anthony Ferner 2024

The right of Anthony Ferner to be identified as the author of
this work has been asserted by Anthony Ferner in accordance
with the Copyright, Designs and Patents Act 1988.

All rights reserved. This book is copyright material and must
not be copied, stored, distributed, transmitted, reproduced
or otherwise made available in any form, or by any means
(electronic, digital, optical, mechanical, photocopying,
recording or otherwise) without the prior written permission of
the publisher.

A CIP catalogue record for this book is available from the
British Library.

1 2 3 4 5 6 7 8 9 10

ISBN 978-1-914148-59-0

www.fairlightbooks.com

Printed and bound in Great Britain

Designed by Sara Wood

Illustrated by Sam Kalda

This is a work of fiction. Names, characters, businesses, events
and incidents are the products of the author's imagination. Any
resemblance to actual persons, living or dead, or actual events
is purely coincidental.

MIX
Paper | Supporting
responsible forestry
FSC® C018072

1. Madrid, 2018

The apartment buildings across the street from our flat have pale pink façades, wrought-iron balconies, high windows and dark-varnished shutters. I watch the occupants, and some stare back. Disapproving, I imagine, of a man in early middle age lounging around and not working. Especially that old woman who comes out onto her balcony directly opposite to water her potted plants. Thin, censorious lips, Franco-era iron-grey helmet of a hairdo, blue-and-white blouse and pearls. (Pearls! On a Monday morning, not even coffee and *tostadas* time.) With her careful, prim mannerisms and her conservative dress sense, she reminds me of my adoptive mother.

I see her most days, the old woman. Normally she's on her balcony, but sometimes I'll spot her coming slowly back from the shops wheeling her wicker basket, anxious at a world that's no longer stable or predictable or white or Catholic and God-fearing, even though it's forty years since Madrid, and Spain, were like that. And I share her fear, not about the Catholic whiteness and all that nonsense, but about the world – Europe, at least – and its stability and predictability.

I don't blame my kids for steering clear of me these past few weeks, Rubén especially. Sara, older, bolder, stroppier, sometimes tiptoes up to the edge, as it were, and peers down into the crater, like she's daring me to erupt; then scurries away again.

Yesterday morning, Margalit came into the living room with a hard expression and said, 'David, I'm going.'

'Going where?'

'Away.' She took a look round the apartment, registering its contents, including me.

'At least tell me...'

She walked to the hall without responding, and went down on one knee to close the zip of a small travel case. I watched the tight curve of her lower back, her hip, the taut flesh of her thigh.

'I don't get it.'

'What is there to get? I've had enough.' She stood up. 'The kids have had enough. Rubén would love to talk to you, but you snap his head off, or he fears you will. He wants his dad back.'

'You can't just leave, I need you here.'

'There's plenty of coffee and cigarettes – that's what you're mainly living off.'

'How will it help,' I said, 'you going?'

She shook her head, gathering force. Walked over to me, heels clicking on the parquet, hands balled. 'You don't talk to me. Don't touch me, don't fuck me. Don't even look at me.'

I didn't look at her.

'You've been wallowing since you got back. I'm sick of it. The kids are sick of it. The world does not revolve around you.'

Her face was lined and her cheeks looked pale and flabby. It shocked me.

She picked up her case. 'You have my number.'

'Just tell me, how long will you be away?'

'I don't know.'

When I first returned home, Margalit tried to get me to explain what I was feeling. I closed up. I thought everything would fall into place. But it hasn't. It's all still churning. I shut my eyes and what I see is the mayhem. Huge seas, flung spray, curtains of water against the bridge windows. The patrol boat, my ship, bucking through, peak to trough. The prospect of ten-metre waves to come. We raced to get hatches closed, lifeboats checked, rations, survival suits, harnesses, jacklines prepared. Heave to, ride it out. Rough, but it should have been fine. The Baltic is hardly the Pacific in typhoon season.

The officer on watch, First Lieutenant Marcelino Feigenbaum – old friend and comrade from naval college – agreed we should cut our speed. Steer into the swell at an angle. We had things under control. The crew went about their business, ashen-faced but efficient. Towards evening, the big waves started to hit. With the seas rolling in heavy and fast from the south-west, we couldn't risk running the troughs, and the waves were too unpredictable to tack. Marcelino went to adjust the steering; he shook his head with his sardonic half-smile, swearing under his breath.

'What's up, Lieutenant?'

'The steering – it's fucked.'

I picked up the telephone, told the chief engineer to start emergency manual steering. The wait, our eyes, mine and Marcelino's, fixed on the rudder-angle indicator, willing it to move. The engineer phoning back: the emergency generator's failing. So the auxiliary steering's also fucked. And that's how it is in my head now. Fucked.

Damn EuDeFor – the European Defence Force, *Force européenne de défense*, *Europäische Friedenskraft*, et cetera, equally useless in a dozen languages. Damn it for its clapped-out fleet, its maintenance backlog, its incompetent bureaucrats. I sent out a distress message, for form's sake, *This is Captain David Aguilera of the ES Pandora...* But they were never going to despatch a rescue mission. So, no choice. At 19:20 hours, I gave the order to

8

abandon ship. Siren blaring, corridor lights strob-
ing. Officers and crew making their way to their
muster stations. The two life rafts launched. The
Pandora doomed.

Rubén wants to know what it was like when
the ship sank. I could have painted a picture for
him, down to the last detail. But it's too raw, he'd
sense my fear. A father is not supposed to be afraid.
I had a well-ordered vessel, a well-drilled crew,
everyone knowing their roles, no panic, just urgent
action. But however many drills you've done, it
doesn't prepare you for that moment. The noises,
the smells. The desolation as the bow finally sinks.
The disorientation as the sea pounds and the winds
deafen you.

So I've put him off with platitudes, or grunts.

I haven't even been able to tell Margalit that the
last thing I did in my cabin on the Pandora, before
putting on my black and red survival suit, was to
seal my personal mobile in the weatherproof inside
pocket of my combat jacket. The phone holding all
I had of her and the kids. Snapshots of better times.
Laughing at home, in a fish restaurant in Madrid, on
holiday in San Sebastián, at a birthday party with
the children. Stepdaughter Sara, part way through
a difficult adolescence, not sure whether to pout or
scowl. Rubén – Rubencito – doggedly faithful, and
still so shy, barely able to look at the camera.

When I finally got back from the Baltic, Margalit wanted me to take up EuDeFor's offer of counselling services. I went along, once. A young guy, must've been barely out of training. Leaning forward, arms on the desk, trying to look authoritative. Patronised me. Spouted clichés about trigger avoidance, addictive behaviours, coping mechanisms. He said, 'I want you to imagine how you'd describe what happened to you, and how you feel about it, describe it to your ten-year-old self, and at the next session I'd like you to say it out loud here. To this cushion.' A cushion! I've heard it's the budget cuts: EuDeFor don't have the resources for one-to-ones with experienced professionals. I got a schoolboy. They also wanted me to join a kind of support group, along with traffic accident and rape victims. For pity's sake!

Last week, Margalit tried one last time.

'David, tell me, what's going on in your mind? You didn't go for counselling, and you might as well still be in the Baltics.'

My only response: to pick up a pack of playing cards and square it aggressively against the tabletop.

She nodded slowly. 'Why are you angry with me?' She leaned her hands on the table. 'You go missing for weeks, no word. Not a sign. Everybody thought you were dead. Me included. Imagine how that was for your children, David. For them, for me. All I knew was your ship had gone down. That's all anyone could tell me. It's like you haven't come home. Just a shell's come back. If anyone has a right to be angry…'

'I know.'

'So talk to me,' she said.

'I'm sorry. It's hard, Margalit.'

I was fidgeting with the deck. She took it from me and set it down on the table. 'Tell me. Please. David?'

She was right, of course. It must have been unthinkably hard for her. But I didn't know how to grasp what I'd felt and been through, the enormity of it, and put it into words. I picked up the pack again and chopped it on the flat of my hand, divided it, shuffled the two parts together, squared the deck and began to lay out rows of cards.

'Solitaire?' she said. 'You're becoming addicted.'

'Oh, for God's sake!'

I threw the half-dealt pack across the table, and it fanned out unevenly. Some cards fluttered to the floor.

She got up and retrieved the fallen cards.

And now she's gone.

'You weren't to blame,' Margalit said, again and again. 'It wasn't your fault. What else could you have done?' She doesn't understand. How could she? Only my friend Feigenbaum, Marce, understands.

I'll go to bed, fall asleep, wake after a couple of hours. Have flashbacks to the stuck rudder-angle indicator, willing it to move; to the wrecked life raft, the lost crew. I can't silence the clatter in my brain. I've been getting up, going to the living-room window, listening to the late-night street noises – the clanking of refuse lorries, the jabber of drinkers spilling out of bars, the woo-woo-woo of ambulances.

Every few days, I've been phoning the naval lawyer I've been assigned, a Dutchman called van Raalte. At the beginning he called me *Day*vid, the English way. 'It's Da*veed* in Spanish,' I'd say, 'Da*veed*. Accent on the second syllable.' But it made no difference, he couldn't get the hang of it. So he's taken to addressing me as 'Captain', which is a relief for both of us. I harangue him regularly on the injustice of my situation. He listens and urges patience: the proceedings can't be hurried, the inquiry will start presently.

When they finally do send for me, I doubt I'll get a fair hearing. I can almost hear those sanctimonious shits shuffling off blame, going on about 'human failures on the ground'.

The flat's filled with the stink of unemptied ashtrays, and a stale smell of beer. I want to stop my marriage, our love, from falling apart. But don't know how. Because the wider world has intruded, like a cannon shell through the hull of a warship.

2.

How can I get across to Margalit what a devastating calamity it is, to lose a ship and most of your crew? The other day, van Raalte described the Pandora as 'only a patrol boat.' *Only.* Okay, so it was worn out, well past its use-by date. But it was the vessel I had command of, along with more than three dozen crew members. I think he was trying to make me feel better. But when you're the one in charge, a sunk patrol boat is as bad as a sunk battlecruiser.

I had the nightmare last night. I'm on the beach, and those black Mitsubishi Warriors are there, and beside them all lined up waiting to be shot, the crew members of the second life raft, Feigenbaum's raft. I try to get up but I can't move, and I'm naked and the militiamen, all in black, see me and start laughing, and come towards me and take aim, and then I wake, crying out. And my wife's not here to calm me.

What else could I have done?

I have visions of us crammed together, the waves pounding, the life raft plunging and rising again and rolling and yawing in the storm, shapes revolving dizzily. I sense still the apprehension of the bodies around me. Hours slipping by since I gave the order to abandon ship, a night come and gone.

My sense of failure is oppressive, especially about what happened to the life raft: The huge wave breaking over us, the awful sound of fabric ripping, a gush of freezing water. I feel sick all over again at the memory of it. A gaping hole, a view of grey skies, heavy seas. Men and women, my crew, flung into the waves. Not even time to catch hold of the webbing of the raft, grasping in vain at deflated strips of fabric. Then, a fierce new wave, we survivors hanging on for dear life in the remaining segment, shivering with fear and shock as much as cold, no one saying a word.

Even here in the flat, as I recall this, see it in my mind, my muscles tense: I wanted to throw myself after them, the lost, but it would have been a meaningless gesture, a suicide by drowning, to no purpose. Intellectually, I grasp that. But it doesn't help. I still don't know what happened to the others. I have to work through all this stuff before I can hope to work through things with Margalit.

The old woman is watering her plants. I nod in greeting. She gives me one of her censorious looks.

I close the shutters and pace the living room. I'm making progress, though: haven't had a beer or a cigarette since Margalit left, and feel the better for it. Yesterday, I cleaned the living room, opened all the windows wide, plumped the cushions, vacuumed, emptied and washed those stinking ashtrays, threw the half-full cigarette packet in the waste bin. I haven't heard from Margalit, but I don't want to contact her until I've got something useful to say.

It's been easy to forget it in these last tetchy weeks, but for me the attraction was instant and enduring. The *flechazo*, the arrow strike. I wouldn't have gone to Carlos's party normally. And she wouldn't have been there either.

I was living on calle Fúcar at the time, near Atocha station. Back then, in 2005, I was a naval officer in training with EuDeFor in its early days. We thought it was a hopeful sign, Europe getting its act together, cooperating to meet the challenges. Now we know better. They had us out at the Naval Academy in Pontevedra. Then they sent us on rotation. I was an intern at the Spanish Ministry of Defence, naval section, bored out of my skull doing desk work; couldn't wait to get back to sea.

I shared a top flat with Marce, a fellow naval trainee. The area had been one of the trendy places during *la Movida madrileña* – the exuberant post-

Franco scene – with the drugs, the punk rock, the mad cafés, Almodóvar. All that stuff. Self-indulgent, over-the-top, undisciplined, but we needed it after the screws loosened. Boy, did my father hate it – my adoptive father, I mean. Dyed-in-the-wool Francoist colonel that he was. By the time I got to calle Fúcar, around 2003 or 2004, droves of tourists were moving in, the old haunts had been replaced with bars trying to be chic, bad music, lurid lighting, ridiculous cocktails, karaoke. Marce and I stuck to the run-down joints, with their tired *bocadillos de tortilla* or *jamón*, TV on in the corner, and the floor ankle-deep in little paper napkins.

Marce would drink his beer, eat his bull's testicles fresh from Las Ventas bullring and spout nonsense. It relaxed me. We were totally different animals, but that's what made our friendship tick. I enjoyed his cynicism; his way of looking at the world with one eyebrow raised, as it were; his bar-room monologues.

'What we're seeing, David,' he'd say, 'are the last thrashings of some puerile do-gooder's vision of a united Europe. The European Union's a failure. And as for EuDeFor, aka WhatTheFuckAreWeFor, look at the state we're in.' He'd already dealt with global warming, large-scale migration, terrorism.

'Another drink, Marce?'

'The European pressure cooker's about to explode, *hermano*. We're heading back to the bad old days of competing nation states. That brilliant model of social organisation that gave us colonial mayhem, two world wars, fascism, the Holocaust, the tragedy of the Balkans… The Baltic states are on a knife edge. Belarus a basket case. Russia dreaming of the greater Empire. Neo-fascists everywhere you look. And so it goes on.' And so he went on.

We'd stare out at the milling groups of foreign trippers gawping in through the bar window like we were cultural exhibits.

'Mass tourism doing its bit for wrecking the planet,' he'd say. 'Not to mention wrecking our city. Our whole continent is turning into a museum for the amusement of visitors from more dynamic places.'

'Didn't you go on a package holiday to Cuba last year?'

'My individual decision makes no difference to—'

'Okay, good to see you take the principled view. Another drink?'

'On the rocks, thanks.'

That flat on Fúcar was great – if you ignored the damp and the cold in winter, the suffocating summer heat, the dodgy plumbing, Marce's tottering piles of books, having to lug gas cylinders up four flights because there wasn't a working lift, the noise from the karaoke bar at all hours.

The lounge had high French windows overlooking the street. Off to one side, Marce's bedroom and a box room; to the other side, a poky kitchen with a tiny window. Marce had this thing about cooking garlic with the skins on. Stank the place out. If you ate one of his stews, the smell stayed on your breath for days.

He'd found the flat – contacts, of course, typical Marce – so he had the big bedroom. I had the box room, with a narrow divan and a fine view of the concrete wall of the interior light well. Still, it was better than the barracks. I covered the bed with a woven wool blanket from the Alpujarras, which some early girlfriend had given me circa 1995. I can hardly visualise her now, but the blanket had nostalgia value.

In the winter, you couldn't get warm. It wasn't just cold, but damp cold, in your bones. More often than not the hot water didn't work so you couldn't take a shower. We'd sit at the round *mesa camilla*, with its electric heating element underneath and the thick tablecloth over our knees to trap the heat. It kept your lower half too hot, while your upper body never warmed up at all. Marce used to say, 'Keeps the balls warm, and the head and heart cold. Ideal combination.'

In those days, Marce was a wiry guy – still is. Light on his feet, laid-back, but with quick, restless eyes. He's the grandson of German Jews who fled Hitler to Argentina, only to find that anti-Semitism was pretty rampant in Buenos Aires, which after the war had its fair share of escaped Nazis and their descendants. When the generals took power in the seventies, his parents fled to Madrid. Marce came over as a one-year-old, so he's basically a Madrilenian, but he's got those Italianate rhythms of Buenos Aires Spanish. I think it's an affectation; he claims it's what he picked up at home. When we lived together he was forever cooking buckwheat groats. He'd toast them in a frying pan then simmer them in chicken stock. Like his German grandmother used to, so he said.

'You go for a piss, and it smells like honeyed earth.'

Perhaps it was the sweet scent that accounted for the stream of women who threw themselves at him. He was convinced his physique, pretty ordinary to be honest, conformed to the golden ratio. That, together with the honeyed smell, gave him the edge.

'I'm sure you're right, Marce.'

'I am right, I've measured it all up, mate. Vitruvian man.'

He'd stand feet together and arms outstretched to the sides. 'Get the aesthetics right, and the erotics will look after themselves.'

To those less naturally gifted – me, for example – he'd give unsolicited advice. 'Look, *hermano*, you're a good-looking guy. No, really. Good bearing, you stand straight, not hunched like all those slouching desk-monkeys.'

'Sure, Marce.'

'You give off an energy, an aura. But get a better haircut. Okay, I know navy regs say it has to be taper-trimmed at the back and blah-blah and all that crap, but hell, man, go to a proper barber for once!'

He stopped to run his hand over his own thread-bare utilitarian buzzcut. 'David, you could smile more. You're too serious. Some women like that, though. They go for the sombre, enigmatic types. And that mischievous grin that outsiders don't get to see, that would tell them you're not quite as reserved and intimidating as you like to make out.'

'Did I ask your advice?'

'No. All the more reason.'

I'd say, 'Shut up for a minute, can't you?' and I'd carry on reading the online training manuals of the European Defence Force.

One evening, he looked at me, eyes narrow, said, 'David, you're coming to a party with me.'

'No I'm not.'

'You've been dumped, you're moping, you need to come out.'

'I wasn't dumped. It was by mutual agreement.'

'Sure. She dumped you, and you agreed. Whatever. The cure for a broken heart is to get straight back in the saddle and—'

'I don't have a broken heart.'

'A bruised ego, then. Either way, I don't want you hanging round the flat infecting it with your bad mood.'

No worse than your garlic skins, I thought.

It was true I'd just been regretfully 'let go' by a woman who worked in personnel at the administrative offices of the Spanish navy. Very pretty, olive-skinned. Too streetwise and experienced for me. We'd only been going out a couple of months, but I guess I was already imagining a future together.

'Fine,' I said, 'if it'll get you off my back.'

So we took the metro up to Nuevos Ministerios. The Saturday night crowd out on the town. Low-paid workers starting their shift or ending it, blank-eyed, like zombies. I was muttering, 'Hate bloody parties. Trivial, time-wasting.'

'That's their whole point, David.'

This particular time-waster was in the flat of Marce's cousin Carlos, who was something in finance. He worked in one of those ugly skyscrapers on La Castellana. Unlike Marce, he did all he could to disguise his Jewish roots. His father, Marce's uncle, had even changed the family name from Feigenbaum to Fernández so he and his kids could 'pass' as insiders.

3.

We got to Carlos's flat around eleven-thirty. He lived on calle Orense, in a soulless apartment block among the soulless shopping centres. Perfect for Carlos. He opened the door, a taller, louder, more expensively tanned and less endearing version of Marce. He ushered us in and jabbed his finger in my direction. 'Another sailor, is he?'

'Yes,' said Marce. 'Another sailor. Now get us a whisky, cousin.'

The flat was full of fake red mahogany furniture. A couple of dozen guests were huddling in noisy cliques in the open-plan living space. Well-dressed, if you like the finance sector high-flyer fashion vibe, the men in expensive Levis and button-down shirts, the women carefully made-up, sleek hair, blonde highlights, gold necklaces, short skirts or low-cut jeans. They'd all be further on in their careers than me. Much better paid, more socially assured.

I hung about on the margins. I'd give it five minutes, for form's sake. Then I'd look for Marce, tell him it wasn't my scene and that I needed an early night. People were starting to dance. Part of me wanted to, but not with this crowd.

On the far side of the room, I spotted another loner, a striking woman with masses of dense, black, corkscrewed ringlets down to her shoulders. Unlike the other expensively underdressed women there, she wasn't openly flaunting her sensuality. She had one arm closed over her chest and was holding a glass of juice. Her solitude was a choice, not the result of social ineptitude. I watched her make her way across the window bay. She looked out to the wet street below, moved on, and stopped again by the floor-to-ceiling bookshelves.

Then she glanced towards me. Maybe she hadn't even seen me, but it felt like she had. It was probably the lighting, but her eyes seemed to glitter. They fixed on me for a moment and darted off. A minute later, she was looking at me again. This time, I looked away.

I moved cautiously round the edge of the room to stand against the bookcase, scanned the books. Mainly self-improving business texts in English or Spanish. *101 Ways to Be a More Effective Dickhead*, that sort of thing. Huddled at the far end of one shelf was a small collection of fiction. Unread, judging by the perfect spines. The author's name on one of the books rang a bell: Juan Carlos Onetti. The book was called *When It No Longer Matters*.

Marce came up to me. 'Can you handle this?' He gestured round at the guests.

'Barely,' I said.

I took the book down from the shelf. Marce saw the title.

'Onetti?'

'Yes. I read one of his I found lying around when we were based in Pontevedra. *The Shipyard*, it was called.'

'Yes, that was my copy.'

'Only read it because of the title. Disappointing.'

'Because?'

'The author isn't remotely interested in shipbuilding.'

'Christ's sake, David, don't be so literal-minded. It's about the human condition.'

'What? Miserable, failed lives trickling away?'

'Yes, the human condition.'

'It just confirmed my prejudice that for reading matter I should avoid novels and stick to naval training manuals.'

'Each to his own. I'm off to throw some shapes.'

I opened the book, scanned a few lines, closed it again. And there she was, the woman, beside me.

'Hi,' she said.

'Hi.'

'You're not interested in *Accounting for Success*?' Her smile was lovely, gentle, with a hint of warm mischief.

'I'm saving that one for later.'

'Of course. So what's this you've got?' Close up, her eyes were beautiful, deep brown and alive. A little sad maybe.

'*When It No Longer Matters*.' I held it up for her to see the cover, and put it down again on a shelf. She was wearing a discreet Star of David on a gold chain round her neck.

'Margalit,' she said, taking my hand. I saw she had a wedding ring. 'Not Margalita or Margarita. Or Marga. Margalit.' It sounded as though it was a clarification she'd had to repeat too often.

'David,' I replied. 'David Aguilera. Good to meet you, Margalit.'

'It always matters, no?'

'I'm sorry?'

'The book title. It always matters, don't you think?'

I felt a shiver. It wasn't flirtatious, not on the surface, but so intimate. She was looking me in the eyes, and this time I didn't look away.

'Which one would you go for?' I said, to break the tension, gesturing towards the books.

'Ah, I'm not particularly interested in novels. It's just that...' She shrugged, and looked round the room at the loud, attention-demanding guests. We glanced at each other and laughed. Out of the corner of my eye, I caught Carlos beckoning me.

'Can I bring you a drink?' I said to her.

'Please. A grapefruit juice, with ice.'

I moved over to Carlos. Marce was standing next to him.

'So you're chatting up *la hebrea*?' said Carlos, topping up my whisky. His hand was steady enough, but his face was flushed.

I stared at him. I didn't like the phrase *chatting up la hebrea*.

'Yes, she's a Jewess, *coño*,' said Carlos. 'She's hot, she's sexy, she's married!' He took a slug of whisky. 'What's not to like?'

'Do shut up, cousin,' said Marce. He could see my irritation, no doubt shared it.

'She's married to a businessman,' said Carlos. 'Jew, naturally. Import–export. My girlfriend's sister works for him.' He laughed. 'He's away on a business trip, the husband. She's on her own. The field is free.'

I looked at him, with military severity. 'I beg your pardon?'

Carlos blinked and tried to smile, but his facial muscles only twitched.

'David.' Marce put his arm on my shoulder. 'Ignore him.' He turned so Carlos couldn't hear and murmured, 'I'm sorry. He's had a skinful.'

As I moved away, glass in hand, I heard Carlos mumble, 'Tasty, that Jewess,' then Marce telling him to shut up. It really bothered me, because Carlos was right. *La hebrea* did provoke lustful thoughts. But only,

I told myself, because there was depth beneath the surface sensuality. Or sensuality lurking in the depths.

I eased my way through the dancers. Marce had now rejoined them. A bit gawky, despite his golden mean dimensions; in rhythm, more or less. I wondered if Margalit had done that thing people do at parties: move on, find someone else to talk to. But she was still by the bookshelves, waiting.

'Shall we sit?' she said.

We went into the study, where the music was less obtrusive, and sat at a small table. Talking, lapsing into silence, talking again, but the silences didn't matter.

I said, 'By your accent, you're not from Madrid. Somewhere southern? Córdoba? Seville?'

'Seville.'

'So what are you doing here?'

'Ah, you know, life throws things, and you dodge.' She offered me a cigarette. I shook my head – I was in one of my abstemious periods. She lit one for herself, looking over at me, and inhaled. I'm sure she was well aware of the effect of her gaze.

'As a matter of fact, Arturo – my husband – brought me to Madrid. The business opportunities are better here. So he says.'

There'd been a barely noticeable pursing of the lips before she'd said the word 'husband'.

'You're Jewish?' I said.

'Yes.'

'Carlos told me. And your necklace.'

'Carlos is an arsehole.'

'Isn't he just.'

As I said this, I found myself touching her lightly on the arm. We smiled at each other. I saw the small gap between her top front teeth. I'm not sure why I found it so attractive. It made me want to kiss her. When she shifted, her body seemed to shimmer, radiate some inner vitality.

'I mean, there are precious few Jews in Spain, right?'

'You'd be surprised. Not many out of the whole population, obviously, but still, tens of thousands.'

I didn't say anything.

She raised an eyebrow. 'What? Now you're going to tell me some of your best friends are Jews. Or you've never met one!'

I blushed and was grateful for the low light. 'Marce, who brought me, is Jewish, and...'

I was going to go on, reveal something about myself, but I stopped mid-sentence. She didn't seem to notice.

'Oh, Marce, he's a heathen!'

She laughed and gestured to the living room.

I looked round. Marce was now dancing with a woman with blonde highlights and exhibitionist earrings: thrusting limbs and shaking hips the pair of them.

'He's a heathen. True.' I laughed too. 'Marce doing what Marce does.'

'Why do people have to take things to extremes?'

'Would you rather go back to Francoist repression?'

'No, obviously not. But look at them all, like dogs sniffing each other.'

'I guess so,' I said, feeling a pang of desire for her.

She made a face. 'I'm only here to say hello to Carlos and my husband's employees. On Arturo's behalf. You know, kiss cheeks, whatever, apologise for his unavoidable absence. Do that, be on my way.'

I took a sip of whisky, and changed the subject. 'You were born here?'

'In Spain? Yes. As were my parents. My family was one of the first to move back to Spain, from Salonica, nearly a century ago. My great-grandparents spoke Greek, and *judeo-español* – Ladino – so it wasn't a problem for them to learn Spanish. The Toledanos. And on my mother's side, the Serfatis, from Morocco.'

'You know your family history.'

'Don't you know yours?'

'Some of it. There's stuff I...' I trailed off.

'I'm a historian by profession, which gives me an advantage in exploring my heritage.'

'A historian?' I'd unconsciously thought of historians as old and hunched, with a gathering layer of dust. Not young and beautiful and vibrant.

'I used to lecture at the University of Seville. But I had to stop when I married.'

'He made you stop?'

'Who? My husband? No!' It was her turn to touch my arm. 'No, this is the twenty-first century, even in the Jewish community of Madrid.' She took a drag on her cigarette and shook her head as she exhaled. 'It's nearly impossible to get a job at a university where you haven't studied and you don't have sponsors. I'll always be a historian. Just not an employed one. I still sit at my computer at home and write. Or hang out in libraries.'

'And I thought you weren't interested in books.'

She put the tip of her tongue, neat and pink, to her upper lip, enjoying the game. 'I said I'm not interested in fiction. I love books about the world we live in. I plan to write one myself, actually. So I have a lot of research to do.'

'A book on?'

'The Sephardi Jews and their host cultures.'

'Okay, that sounds… highbrow.'

'Not really. I foresee mega-sales, film star status.'

'Uh-huh.'

We grinned at each other, complicit.

'I'm very fond of the National Library,' she said, 'It has an awesome reading room.'

'The National? On Recoletos? I've never been inside.'

'You should. It has marvellous sloping desks covered in green baize and in the afternoon you can lay your head on your arms for five minutes and take a little siesta. I manage to sleep through the faint sounds of disapproval from elderly gentlemen readers.'

I chuckled, enjoying the image of her lovely dark hair spread across the green of the library desk. A wavy sea of hair.

'What about you, David? I've been doing most of the talking.'

'What would you like to know?'

'I sense you don't haunt libraries as a rule.'

'Correct. I'm a naval officer.'

She raised her eyebrows, in surprise, I think, not disapproval.

'Was on a warship in the North Atlantic, currently stationed in Madrid.'

'In Madrid,' she said. 'Curious.'

'I'm on detachment at naval headquarters in the Ministry of Defence. Which is round the corner from the National Library as it happens.'

We carried on chatting a while longer, until she frowned and glanced at her watch and said she should go and talk to Arturo's employees. I felt disappointed; there'd been something more going on than an agreeable chat at a party. I was afraid I'd miss my opportunity.

'Meet for lunch, maybe,' I said, trying to sound casual, and failing. 'I mean, we're so close. One of these days. Or would that...?'

Her face was in shadow and I couldn't tell if she was grimacing or smiling. She was probably too used to corny lines like that. I swirled the melting ice cubes. They clinked against the side of the glass. I was wishing I'd kept my mouth shut.

'I suppose we could discuss our mutual interest in the non-fiction sections of libraries,' she said. She opened her purse, took out a pen and scribbled her number on a scrap of paper. 'Message me. I may or may not answer.'

'Understood.'

We stood up and touched lips to cheeks. She made her way back through the partygoers with a swaying walk that managed to be both modest and alluring.

4.

It was two when I left the party. I edged past a drunken Carlos, said a quick, 'Thank you, I'm off.' Carlos tugged at my arm. 'Did you pull? Did you pull *la hebrea*?'

I bristled, gave him my steely gaze. He failed to take the hint and laughed, an irritating little guffaw. '*Macho*, don't take it personally, anyone would think you're one of the brotherhood.' He was very drunk, slurring his words, but he must have known he was going to trigger a response. 'Sorry, sorry, I should be careful what I say.' He held out his hand in a placatory gesture.

I ignored the hand and went towards the front door. Carlos called out behind me, 'Ha! Nice bit of kosher meat, no?'

He's a Jew himself, for pity's sake, even if he pretends not to be. I turned, strode back and put my hand against the wall, impeding his escape.

'I didn't quite catch what you just said.'

'Hey, it was a joke. Don't you have a sense of humour?'

Someone called, 'Guys! Cool it!' I relaxed my posture, patted Carlos on the neck, and muttered, '*Tranquilo, macho*, calm down, nothing's going to happen.'

Carlos squealed, 'Who the fuck does he think he is!'

Marce hurried over.

'Doesn't he get irony?' Carlos said. 'Next time, cousin, leave him at home. Fuck's sake!'

Marce shook his head. 'You were being ironically offensive, is that it? You never learn.'

It was a relief to be outside in the drizzle, to cool down and collect my thoughts. I'd missed the last metro. I could have taken a cab but I was too hyped up. I decided to walk. It's something I like to do when I'm out in Madrid at night: soaking up the smells and sounds, unwinding. I reckoned it would take fifty minutes if I marched it. Malasaña was buzzing, neon glistening off wet pavements, and there were still drinkers on the rooftop bar of Bellas Artes. I had this shivery unease, like early symptoms of flu. But I knew it wasn't flu.

I got home dog-tired, feeling like I'd been on a fifty-kilometre training hike across the Picos de Europa. My brain was too full of images of Margalit and her smile and her warm voice and the way she moved. I must have dozed off eventually because at five in the morning I was woken by jangling keys, stage-whispering, the front door banging. Marce returning from the party accompanied, I guessed, by the woman with blonde streaks in her hair. My mouth felt parched.

Later that morning, over coffee and toast, Marce said, 'You gave Carlos a hard time. Defending her honour, very creditable.'

'I didn't do anything. Had a friendly word with him.'

'But, hey, did you ask yourself what she'd have made of all that straining anger?'

'I wasn't straining. I was quite relaxed, actually. He wasn't, it's true.'

Marce's reproach about Carlos stung. Maybe Margalit wasn't looking for a knight errant charging to her defence. Though what *was* she looking for? A little something on the side when her husband was out of town? I doubted that.

'So,' I said, to change the subject. 'You didn't come home alone from the party?'

Marce smiled. 'Correct. Two beautiful moths fluttering against each other in the depths of the night and, come morning, they go their separate ways.'

'Don Juan Feigenbaum, so poetic, as always.'

He laughed.

'She's Jewish,' I said.

'Who's Jewish?' he said, feigning ignorance.

'The woman I was talking to at the party. Margalit.'

'Yes, and?'

I shook my head. 'And nothing.'

Marce's bedroom door opened. The blonde-streaked woman emerged. She gave her hair a quick fluff-up with her fingers. 'Sofi,' she said and held up her hand to me. I nodded. She came and kissed Marce on the lips, drew back and kissed him again. She said, 'See you later, Marce, *mi amor*,' and was gone.

A few days after the party, I called Margalit. I was shaky with nerves.

She said, 'So you were *defending my honour.*'

'What? At the party? I'm sorry, I was just... I know I should have ignored him.'

'Don't apologise, David. He thinks he's being clever and that saying he's being ironic excuses the bullying. Anyway, I quite like the idea you scared him witless.'

'I didn't mean to...'

'Ah, but all that latent physical menace. Something raw and unfiltered about it, maybe. I'm not a fan of violent men, obviously. But I sense you know how to control a capacity for violence.'

'You're calling me raw and unfiltered?' I said.

She laughed. 'Yes. Like the best virgin olive oil.'

'Okay.'

She wasn't bothering to hide her interest in me. I felt heady, heard myself make strange little embarrassed noises.

'So,' she said, to put me out of my misery, 'what did you phone for, David?'

'Oh, nothing, not really,' I stammered. I recovered enough to say, 'I was just wondering...'

'Yes?'

'Would you like to go for a drink?'

'Oh, gosh,' she said slowly, as if she hadn't seen it coming.

'But it doesn't matter if you're busy, you said you might not be able to—'

'Yes. Fine. I could manage that.'

I was so startled she'd said yes that I only managed to say, 'Oh.'

'As long as the violence is only latent. I don't much care for bloodshed in bars.'

She sounded like she was smiling at the other end of the line, and that stopped me making a complete arse of myself.

'No bloodshed,' I said.

5.

Quick kisses to cheeks. Hands briefly on shoulders. I caught a subtle perfume I didn't recognise, her own delicious warm smell, a hint of cigarette smoke. I felt heady, and so nervous I thought I'd dry up altogether.

'What are you having?'

'I'll have what you're having,' she said.

She was wearing a dark blue dress, that's all I noticed about what she had on. Jewellery? A necklace? I'm not even sure about the Star of David. Earrings? I think so. The dress showed the curve of her hips, the soft swell of her stomach.

The bar was nondescript, some other customers but not too busy. We wouldn't attract attention. We talked about ourselves and each other, and Madrid and the sea, and her history projects.

She told me she'd not wanted to go to the party, and I said, me neither.

'I'm a married woman, and I should have been at home with my toddler. But Arturo is "away"'

– she made inverted commas with her fingers – "travelling". That's what he calls it, but we both know what it means. He wanted me to go because several of his employees would be there. Contacts, *networking*, he calls it, like I'm his ambassador.'

I said, 'I'm not following you, Margalit.'

She took a breath and said, 'My husband is not into women. My husband's into men, that's why he…'

I must have looked shocked. 'Why couldn't he just come out as gay, and save everybody a lot of grief? These days, people don't bat an eyelid at the idea of gays in the navy, even.'

'You don't understand. That's not how things are done in our community. The cultural pressures can be crushing. We feel under siege. Marriage failure is a threat to the group. So you don't talk about such things. Though it's always there, like a vague shape you sense in the room in the dark, and everyone's terrified to put the light on.'

I was going to ask why in that case they'd got married in the first place but it was probably not the moment.

I said, 'Let's have another gin-tonic.'

'I'll drink to that!' She clinked glasses with me.

'What do you write about?' I asked, searching for safer ground.

'The Sephardis. What happened to them after they were expelled from Spain. Their Jewish culture, how it intertwined with that of the host lands that took them in.'

Her eyes kept focused on mine. 'Spain – *Sefarad* – was like their promised land.'

'It's been a long wait since they got kicked out.'

'That's true, but what's a mere 500 years in the history of the Jews!' She laughed, a beautiful melodic chime of a laugh. 'The idea of *Sefarad* kept them going in exile. They took the keys of their houses, and dreamed of returning. Do you know that poem by Borges?'

I shook my head, of course, feeling ashamed at my ignorance. Perhaps Marce would know the poem. 'Borges...' I echoed, stupidly.

'The one that goes on about Abarbanel, Farías and Pinedo,' said Margalit, 'about how they still had a key to their house in Toledo. The poem's called "A Key in Salonica", so it has a special meaning for me.'

'Do you still have a key in the family?'

'Not as far as I know. It's a notion more than a reality, I suspect. Symbolising the attachment to *Sefarad*. And a few centuries later, we started trickling back. So here we are. I want to fill in some of the gaps in the story that hasn't been fully told, that's still unfolding.'

'Towards?' I asked.

She tilted her head and blew out a long stream of smoke that lost its form and curled up towards the ceiling, bluish in the lights of the bar. 'Who knows?

Another age of flourishing culture, like in the glory days of *Sefarad*. Or more catastrophe, another holocaust.'

I took a sip of my gin-tonic. '*Caramba*, is the outlook that grim?'

'Well look around you, David. Europe's not doing great, is it? You should know that as a naval man.'

I nodded.

'And the Jews are the canaries in the coal mine when the madness begins.'

'*Canaries?*' I said.

'You know what I mean.'

'The Jews are scarcely the only canaries.'

She sighed, as if she heard the line all the time, *the Jews aren't special, the Jews are this, the Jews are that*. 'Well maybe,' she said. 'But it's my lived experience. I have to start with what I know. And who I am. When I was a kid, people would still say "*es un judío*", "he's a Jew". Meaning someone's a nasty, grasping piece of work.'

'Really?' I didn't mean it to come out as sceptical as it sounded.

'When you're brought up a Catholic, you don't see this stuff. You certainly don't experience it.'

I said, 'I'm not actually...' and tailed off, uncomfortable.

'Even educated people, professionals, would say *judío* as a term of contempt. I once heard a professor in the university casually say it.'

'And now?'

'Now it's more hidden, a more *respectable* kind of anti-Semitism.'

I winced. Was she about to go on about Israel and the Palestinians? I wanted to change the subject. I said, 'And your family came to Spain from Salonica?'

'Yes. In the 1920s mainly, and some after the war. But Salonica was as important to them as *Sefarad*, I think. My grandparents often talked of going back to Salonica. It's funny, you know. They were very home-sick for a place they'd never lived in. It's like we Jews need this sense of exile, we always feel we ought to be someplace else. Some of their cousins did return to Salonica, actually. Like my great-aunt Roza, who only left during the war and went back afterwards.'

She drew on her cigarette again, half-closed her eyes. 'I imagine Salonica in the old days as a city of light and arts and commerce, a great port, different cultures prospering alongside each other.'

'It probably wasn't ever like that.'

'Maybe not. But I'd love to go there some day, see for myself.'

'You've never been?'

'Not yet. But I will.'

We ordered another round of drinks.

She said, 'Now, tell me more about you, David.'

So I told her about my naval career, my hopes for EuDeFor, my love of the sea, my different postings. My excitement over a possible stint in the Mediterranean. She had to lean forward to catch my words. I must have been speaking low, making an effort to soften my voice, which I know can sound harsh and intimidating. She was looking at me and we held each other's gaze and there was a silence, a sense of things about to happen. I felt heady from the gin-tonic, the conversation, the closeness.

She said gently, 'What are you thinking?'

I did that thing I do in social situations, when I'm unsure of my ground, of swirling the ice cubes in my glass. I felt I was about to leap off a cliff. 'I'm thinking...' I said, and I stopped and shook my head. 'No, it's okay.'

'Please, say what you were going to say.'

I took a breath and puffed it out. 'I was thinking I'd like us to sleep together.'

'Oh, okay. Well, well.' She bit her lip.

'I mean, not tonight, that's probably not a good idea, but maybe at some point, but soon... I'm sorry.'

I ground to a halt. I stared at the bottles glinting behind the bar, blue and silver and golden. I felt those bottles would always be etched into my memory of the moment.

She held up her right hand to show the gold wedding ring. 'I am married, as you know. And I have a baby daughter.'

'Yes,' I grinned, 'but that's fine with me.'

She looked back at me, unsmiling.

'I'm sorry,' I said, 'I shouldn't have asked.'

'Yes,' she said firmly. 'I mean, yes, I'd like that.'

'But you're married,' was all I could say.

She smiled and put her hand over mine. 'And I'm Jewish.'

I looked at her and murmured, surprised at myself and also horrified at letting my guard down further: 'So am I.'

'You?' she said, stunned. She raised a quizzical eyebrow at me as if to say why hadn't I mentioned anything about my Jewishness at the party. I'd been about to then, but I hadn't felt ready.

'Yes,' I said. 'My mother is Jewish.'

She didn't take her hand from mine but in the dark recess of the bar, by now almost deserted, she leaned forward and touched her lips to mine. Her lips were soft and sweet, and when she leaned forward again we kissed, properly, deeply, and it was like a heavy swell at sea, awe-inspiring and invigorating, and a touch scary.

6.

The ringing of my mobile jolts me out of my thoughts about the early days. It's van Raalte, my navy lawyer. Matters are advancing, he says, and I'll be called back to Kiel soon, to EuDeFor naval headquarters, to be questioned about the loss of the Pandora.

Of course, Marce and I had a thorough debrief when we finally made it back to Germany after walking across half of Lithuania and a good chunk of Latvia to escape. But these things drag on. Van Raalte advises me to have our story clear, maybe make detailed notes of what happened. I say I have something written down. *Good*, he says.

'I'm not in the dock, am I? This is an inquiry, not a trial.'

'Yes, of course. But the optics are also important. You want to come out of it looking good.'

'I'm getting flashbacks,' I say. 'Finding it hard to sleep.'

'Have you tried sleeping pills?' he asks.

Even when I'm awake, I get the images, on repeat. The Pandora going down, of course. The wrecked life raft. Being thrown by the waves onto the strand. The howl and whine of the wind through the trees where I lie hidden from the militias. My injured leg, stabbing like knives, oozing pus. Some local woman taking me in – Kamilė. Her scent, mixed with tobacco smoke, pine needles. Who knows why she helped me? From the goodness of her heart, I think. Maybe also from loneliness; the militia had shot her husband. She found me in the pine wood. I remember, in the distance, a few houses, red-tiled roofs, night closing in...

My body's tensing up, my pulse starting to race. I know I lost days in a fever, and more days recovering my strength. When I was better, Kamilė pressed some cash and a parcel of food – bread and a large hunk of salami – into my hand, and she reached out and touched my cheek with her fingers, nothing more.

'So,' van Raalte says, 'you got separated from the crew of your life raft. Half of them dead anyway.'

'Yes. Got the crew safely into the life rafts, everything by the book. But my raft ripped on some sunken hazard. Came ashore on the Spit. We clawed our way out of the wreckage. No evidence of the lost crew, not even washed up bodies.' I'd vomited on the sand when I'd realised we wouldn't find them again.

'The...' – he hesitates, consulting his notes, presumably – '...Curonian Spit?'

'Yes. The Curonian Spit. A hundred kilometres of sand dune, basically.' No hard edges, no rocky bays or headlands, no cliffs. No hiding places. A road along it, a few trees. To the west, the Baltic Sea, to the east a huge lagoon, tens of kilometres wide. 'Northern half Lithuanian, southern half Kaliningrad.'

'Russian?'

'Yes, the Russian enclave. Home to Russia's Baltic fleet. Sensitive area. And we beached in the wrong part.'

'So you head north, up the Spit.'

'Yes. Without my crew, because the storm separated us.' I'd gone back into the raft to retrieve provisions when a rogue wave hit and took me back out to sea, and when I came ashore again, there was no sign of the others.

'So you're alone. And you stumble across the crew of the second life raft, Lieutenant Feigenbaum's life raft, on the beach. Being held at gunpoint by a militia group?'

'Yes. Nothing I could do. Also, I had a gashed leg.'

'I see. So you escaped into the woods, is that right, and this local woman took you in, dealt with the leg?'

'Yes.'

'You stayed a few days, and then made for the ferry at Klaipeda, at the northern end of the Curonian Spit?'

'Correct. '

'You've no idea what happened to the crew after you saw them?'

'No. No idea.'

I was devastated, miserable, alone. Grieving for my lost crew. Constant Russian patrols on the Spit road. My phone finally out of battery, and Margalit almost an abstraction, a ghost, an absence; a Penelope to my Odysseus, as Feigenbaum would no doubt have pretentiously put it. It was cold, early October, night had fallen. I got to the ferry and paid for a one-way trip. The woman in the ticket office pointed to the line of foot passengers. I waited with them until the ferryman unhooked the chain and allowed us aboard, together with a few cars and vans. I climbed the steps to the passenger deck. In front of me, a man. Oddly dressed in combat trousers and a brown, knee-length quilted jacket. The man turned to look over the rail at the water as the ferry began to move. His face was unshaven and thin.

It was Feigenbaum. Marce.

My heart, as they say, leapt. An ally, a friend. Together, we might just make it.

'And you bumped into Lieutenant Feigenbaum completely by chance, at this ferry?' says van Raalte.

'Correct.'

'Hmm. Another strange, if not far-fetched, coming together of circumstances one might say.'

'Even so, that's what happened. Not *far-fetched*, since that's the only way to the north from the Spit. Unless you swim.'

'Perhaps you do not use that phrasing to the tribunal,' van Raalte says.

Far-fetched or not, it was him, Marce. I leaned on the rail, watching the lights on the water. I said, 'Don't react, don't look round.' His body stiffened. '*Joder!*' he muttered. 'You scared me out of my fucking wits!' He took a long drag of his cigarette, flicked the still-glowing butt into the sea, blew out the smoke which curled up into the darkness. 'Man,' he murmured, 'am I pleased to see you.'

But how will all that help me at the Kiel inquiry? Or with Margalit? She already thinks Marce and I are closer in some things than she and I are.

Thinking of Kamilė still gives me a pang of guilt. Nothing happened between us, but if I'd stayed longer, something would have. There was a definite attraction. I was alone, and she was alone, and there was the sheer joy of being alive when I could have died of sepsis if she hadn't found me, or been shot by some marauding Russian patrol.

I end the call with van Raalte, irritated by the man, though he's only doing his job. I wonder how Margalit is. Just getting on with life without me, I imagine. Being there for the kids, trying to soften the disruption to their lives. Busy with her research at the National Library, putting the finishing touches to the book she's been writing on the Sephardis. Perhaps thinking about me, about us, whether we have a future.

It was all so heady in our early days. I try to trace it out, hoping some golden thread will reconnect me to what we felt then. I didn't go to bed with her that first night, after the drinks in the bar. A sense of decorum held us back. But the delay just helped build the tension. I couldn't settle to anything. Certainly not to EuDeFor training manuals, even with exams coming up. A couple of days later I got a text: *What are you doing tonight?*

We went for dinner.

When dinner was finished she took me back to her flat. Her toddler was staying with the mother-in-law, Arturo's mother.

We were shy with each other at first.

'It's been a while,' she said, and smiled ruefully.

She took us past the conjugal bedroom to the spare room – some residual delicacy about her marriage, I suppose. But once we were there, all her hesitancy, our hesitancy, dissolved. Coming together seemed natural, like rain on parched land. Afterwards, we lay in each other's arms, smiling, not speaking.

7.

In the morning, we awoke, entwined, and I felt the warmth of her body and had a sense of calm and well-being so unfamiliar it was disturbing.

That was the start. In the happy, mostly carefree early days, we'd sometimes stay in bed for much of the weekend, making love. I was embarrassed by my libido.

'It's on account,' I'd say. 'For when I'm at sea.'

She'd tease me and play with me, and go, '*Firme, marinero!*' – 'Attention, sailor!' – and when I duly got hard again, she'd whisper into my ear, 'I like lust; lust makes me feel alive.' She made sure I took account of her needs and desires and she'd tell me or show me what she wanted, without bruising my male ego. She got me to loosen up in bed, until I could laugh at the undisciplined messiness of sex. I suppose I'd always taken it with a pained sacramental solemnity – the Catholic background, no doubt.

'Hey,' she'd say, 'you come and sleep in the wet patch. You're the sailor!'

'I don't remember anything about that in the Code of Conduct for EuDeFor Naval Officers.'

'Section 42. Protection of the Dignity of Women.'

A few months into our relationship, we came to the conclusion that we needed to be together. I felt daunted by the magnitude of the decision, but I knew it was right for me, for both of us. I gave up my flat share in calle Fúcar, and we moved into a three-bedroomed apartment with a balcony, in Chamberí – which is still our apartment, scarily empty now without her and the kids. The rent took up two-fifths of my salary, but my adoptive mother helped with the deposit.

A couple of years after the move, Rubencito was born. I didn't anticipate the sheer delight of fatherhood. Within seconds of seeing the small ugly thing, with its greasy, whitish coating, on Margalit's breast, I was in love with it. It changed the dynamics in the family. Sarita, who was three when Rubén was born, soon realised he wasn't just an unwelcome visitor but a permanent fixture, and that I was infatuated with him.

Margalit supplemented our income with some freelance work as a copy-editor of long and boring historical volumes. In the evenings, she'd sit in the small study surrounded by reference books, and point the flexible aluminium lamp at her papers.

'The Carlist Wars will keep me in work for the next decade,' she'd say.

The harsh lighting strained her eyes, and she'd fall asleep at the desk, her head on her folded arms. I'd go and lean over her, part her hair and kiss the delicate spot on the nape of her neck. She'd wake with a start, smile at me and draw my face to hers for a kiss.

'Come to bed,' I'd say, 'while the baby's still asleep.'

'I'll just finish this section and I'll join you.'

She'd probably be up half the night, going beyond the call of duty to make sure her line edits were comprehensive and unchallengeable.

'I hope you're learning a lot of history at least.'

'You have to concentrate so hard word by word you often don't see the wood for the trees. But I've learned more than I thought I needed about Zumalacárregui.'

'You do realise your pay rate is now approximately one euro fifty an hour.'

She'd poke her tongue out at me and carry on, running her finger along the line of text on the screen. I encouraged her to do the work, because it was good for her as well as for the household budget. When I was on shore leave, I helped out more with Rubén. I learned – to my astonishment – how to change his nappy, a procedure that, according to Margalit, I planned with military precision. At night, when she was so tired she often didn't hear the baby's cries,

I'd get up and bottle-feed him with breast milk she'd expressed the day before. And when she went on research trips to archives in Córdoba or Seville, I'd take over the running of the household and felt proud that few disasters occurred.

Marce, of course, would make pointed remarks about the feminisation of the male identity and what he called 'infantile enslavement', by which he meant subjugating one's own interests to the demands of small children.

'The apparently powerless one is hence the all-powerful in this arrangement. I'm surprised you accede to it so readily, David.'

'I'm merely helping in the production of a next generation that will – one hopes – be less dysfunctional than ours.'

But the truth was that I loved caring for Rubén, felt happy in my skin for once, could let my guard down.

Margalit and I had a few practical difficulties to overcome. Like dealing with Arturo's reaction when she told him she was leaving him. He wouldn't agree to grant her a *get*, a religious divorce, and created problems over child maintenance, though he accepted that she would have Sara. The girl would have been a hindrance to him.

'The community sees me as a wicked ball-breaking Jewess,' said Margalit, 'who forced my husband to seek consolation in the arms of other men.'

'Poor guy. It must have been a challenge to service you on your wedding night. But if duty calls…'

She grimaced. 'Our wedding night was something else. We made love once then, and twice more in all the time we were together, the last occasion being when I fell pregnant with Sarita. If you can call it making love. Face-to-face, strangely. I don't exactly have the girlish figure that might have passed muster, not with my hips and tits.'

'I just love them,' I said.

'Yes, darling, I know you do.' She kissed me. 'His eyes were like glazed over. When he was coming, he bared his teeth like an angry primate. Gave a little grunt, like *urgh*, and he had this look, like he'd eaten a cockroach or something.'

She laughed at the grotesque image, and I joined in, a little guiltily.

'I didn't understand it then, though now of course I do. As you say, it must have been difficult for him. He was at a gay club the evening before our engagement party.'

'Seriously?'

'No, I swear, there were eyewitnesses, a gay couple, friends of mine.'

'Why did you go ahead and marry him?'

'Good question. A combination of things. I didn't want to admit to myself he was gay, though I did suspect that he was.' She chewed the flesh round her fingernail. 'I must have known, though. The way he'd eye up the catering staff when we went to weddings or bar mitzvahs. Flirt with the waiters, you know. I should have realised. He was a good-looking guy, not some golem, so there was that – I thought we'd make a handsome pair, I suppose. And he was well off. So there was the financial security side of things. And parental pressure. From my side and his. They wanted to get him married off as soon as possible, for obvious reasons. Also, I was a bit rebellious, wanted to leave home, you know, lose my virginity.'

'Rebellious? And I'm the beneficiary.'

'You could say that.' She pondered my remark. 'Maybe it's because of my grandfather Isaac, the one who fought with the Greek partisans in the Second World War. He used to tell me stories about his exploits when I was a kid. A very magnetic guy. He'd say, "Always, *always*, you have choices".'

'And you chose me, *mi amor*.'

'Yes, and you chose *me*!'

8.

I'm sitting at the kitchen counter, jotting down notes for van Raalte. Mainly it's trying to get the sequence of events right. Apart from the big incidents, the traumatic flashback stuff, it blurs into the long, tedious process of putting one foot in front of another until we were exhausted enough to drop. Of sleeping in barns, hiding in ditches, foraging for enough food to keep us going for another day.

The phone rings. Van Raalte, naturally.

'Tell me about the European Defence Force, Captain,' he says.

'EuDeFor? Why?'

'Background, Captain. Context. You keep telling me EuDeFor is a failing organisation. That they gave you an unreliable vessel, that if they had been competent, your boat would not have sunk, that—'

'Okay, okay. I joined as a trainee naval officer back in the noughties, not long after it was set up. All I know is it was meant to stiffen Europe's resolve and bolster its eastern flanks. Much good did it do us. I mean, things were unravelling, the Russians were meddling, Turkey was poking away at the migrant crisis. But it built on existing structures.'

'Meaning what?'

'That there was informal cooperation going back years before all that. Exchanges of personnel, joint patrols, exercises. So EuDeFor already existed, embryonically at least.'

'I see. And the formal organisation was set up, what, seventeen, eighteen years ago?'

'I guess so.'

He's obviously reading from notes, or maybe Wikipedia: '"EuDeFor was formally established at the Vienna conference of 2000, ratified by seventeen countries at the Riga Treaty of—"'

'Whatever. You obviously know more about it than I do, *Licenciado*. I'd just add that it wasn't given enough resources from the start to do its job properly. And the political infighting at the top levels doesn't help.'

'You have evidence of that?'

'It's widely recognised.'

'That's… helpful.'

I make my excuses and put the phone down. There's only so much of van Raalte's pedantic lawyerliness I can stand. All I know is EuDeFor has never not been in crisis.

As I'm ending the call, the front door opens, and Sara comes in. I haven't seen her since they all left.

'*Hola,*' I say.

She grunts.

'Are you all right?' I ask, 'Do you need something?'

'Not from you,' she says, and disappears into her bedroom.

I can hear her talking on her mobile, animated and laughing, probably mocking me and my many failings. After a few minutes, she re-emerges carrying a small bag and marches down the hall, her expression severe again, not looking in my direction. The front door opens and closes. I, of course, am the one to blame for the upending of her life, and with her adolescent slyness she knows how to make me pay. Margalit would say, 'Calm down, David, she's still a child.'

From our early days together, Margalit would ask me about my own family. She'd work away at my reticence. 'David, think of me as the dentist. I'm going to pull your teeth out one by one. No anaesthetic.'

I'd wince.

'Look, darling, like it or not it's part of who you are, I'm not going to judge you for it.'

Bit by bit, she extracted information. Difficult for me, painful. I didn't know when she'd stop tugging.

'Start with your parents, darling, and go from there.'

I opened my mouth but couldn't get words out. It really was like being at the dentist. She'd wait patiently. 'So you were adopted?'

'Yes, *cariño*, but there's a lot I still don't understand.'

'Not talking about it won't help you understand it better.'

On one occasion, in those snug, confessional moments after sex, she said, 'How old were you when you found out?'

'Fifteen, I guess. The day of my fifteenth birthday in fact.'

'What?' she said. 'They just came out with, "Hey, Davidcito, you're adopted, man, *felicidades!*"?'

'Something like that. But it wasn't unexpected, somehow. I always had the feeling I was different.'

'In what way *different*?'

'Oh, you know. Taller. Better-looking.'

'And modest with it, no?'

We laughed, and she kissed me.

'And,' I said, 'they both had little black eyes, like black peas, and hardly any neck. I suppose that wasn't their fault.'

'So what happened?'

'My mother called me in. Afternoon of my birth-day. Almost like a job interview. My father was already waiting for me at the dining table. She said, "Darling, there is something we need to say to you. You're old enough to know. You realise we both love you very much," or words to that effect. My father was trying and failing to be informal – he had a cravat on instead of a tie. A fixed grin that was meant to be a sympathetic smile.'

'Maybe it really was sympathetic, *cariño*.'

'Anyway, awkward silence, then he goes, "Rocío, let's get on with it, woman." So my mother sighs and clasps her hands to her chest and says, "I am not your birth mother." Then she pants as if she's run up five flights of stairs. I go, "How do you mean?" She says, "Your biological mother couldn't keep you. So I became your mother. When you were a few weeks old."'

'So how did you feel?' Margalit asked.

'Like a sinkhole just opened up, and...' I stopped, bit my lip.

'What happened then, *cariño*?' Margalit stroked my hair and nuzzled into me. 'Tell me.'

'My father comes out with, "Legally, you are as much our son as if we were your natural parents."'

'*Legally*? How empathetic! What did you say?'

'I lost it. Shouted at them for not telling me before. Father said, "We're telling you now, and you will mind your tone with your mother." I remember screaming, "She's not my real mother and you're not my father, and no wonder I don't fit into this bloody family!"'

Perhaps that's how Sara feels, that she doesn't fit into this bloody family any more when I'm around.

'Did your father send you to your room after your outburst?'

'Strangely, I can't now remember. Maybe he went easy on me because it was my birthday. Though that didn't usually stop him.'

Margalit chuckled. 'Was he the kind to say *it's for your own good, son*?'

'Not even. He didn't feel the need to justify himself to me like that.'

'Well, you turned out okay.' She kissed my cheek, her arm round my shoulder. 'What else?'

'That was it, really. I said to Rocío, "What about my *real* mother? Where is she?"'

'Which must have hurt her,' said Margalit.

'I guess. But I was upset and angry. All she'd tell me was that my "biological" mother was a young woman who couldn't keep me because of certain complications she couldn't go into, and I'd have to ask my father. I knew he wouldn't tell me anything. I said I wanted to meet her, my real mother. She said, "That's not possible, darling. You won't find her because there're no records." I said, "I don't believe you. There's got to be records." She started crying and I ran to my bedroom and sobbed and beat the pillow and banged my head against the headboard.'

'Come here,' Margalit said, and she held me tight and stroked my face.

'It's hard work, going over it all. Hard bloody work.'

'Of course it is,' she said. 'So once it had all sunk in, what did you do with that knowledge?'

I pulled away from her and scratched my chin, trying to recapture my reactions at the time. 'Of course, at one level I already knew. But this was the official confirmation. I dwelt on it a lot, agonised about it, went through a phase of wanting to become a priest. Which is a bit perverse as I was also rejecting Catholicism as a teenager.'

'Sorry, darling, you are not priestly material. Rocío must have been delighted though, being such good buddies with Father Ignacio and all that.'

'No, she hated the idea and did her best to dissuade me, which only made me keener. I remember saying to her, "Is it because you won't have grandchildren?" Pretty mean, no?'

'Yes, it was.'

Margalit was gazing at me with her eyes half-closed, a sort of teasing, sensual interrogation. 'So tell me, why didn't you become a priest?'

'I knew deep down it wasn't for me, that I wasn't a believer. Father Ignacio could see that too.' I hesitated. 'And girls, I suppose.'

'You're not blushing, are you, *mi amor*?'

'No, the aircon needs adjusting.' We grinned at each other. 'And later, of course, came the whole Jewish thing.'

I wish Margalit was here with me now, stroking my face, easing the pain. But obviously she can't be, by virtue of the fact that I'm the cause not only of my pain, but hers too. And Sara's, and Rubencito's.

9.

My disapproving neighbour is on her balcony again, flapping away at the pigeons. She's dressed with even greater care than usual: patterned blouse, three rows of pearls, and some concoction on her head in what looks like red velvet. It could be it's her homage to Franco's wife, Carmen. My adoptive father always used to mark important dates in the Francoist calendar. Like the 18 July fiesta commemorating the beginning of the 'Glorious Uprising'. Even after the public holiday was abolished, Don Rafa carried on celebrating it. He'd put on a suit and tie, smoke a cigar and phone his old army chums, signing off with grunted slogans like *Viva España! Una, Grande y Libre! Viva!* I'd keep out of the way in my bedroom, hoping he wouldn't summon me for a brandy-scented lecture on the dictator's achievements. Rafa expected his wife to dress smartly too on these occasions, even if she wasn't leaving the house and nobody except him and me would be seeing her. 'Rocío, *mujer*, it's a matter of basic respect,' he'd growl, and she'd sigh and comply.

Rocío got to see Rubencito as a baby. With prompting from Margalit, I took him for her to coo over. She clasped her hands and asked to hold him, something she probably wouldn't have dared to do had Rafa still been alive. When she'd put him back in his pushchair she turned and hugged me, rubbing my cheek with her hand. If only she'd been that affectionate when I was a young boy.

'My grandson. You don't know how happy it makes me, David! I want you to promise to send me photos. And bring him to see me again.'

After my adoptive father had died, Rocío had come more into her own – taking charge of Rafael's funeral arrangements, telling the priest, Father Ignacio, what to say in the oration, staying calm and dignified at the service, though it must have been an ordeal. At the graveside, with the priest droning on about '*absolve vinculis delictorum*', she lifted her black veil to wipe her eyes with a handkerchief. She shrugged off the comforting arms of female relatives and clutched me close.

A few days after the funeral, when I was getting ready to return to my posting in Las Palmas, Rocío sat me down at the table, unlocked a small box and took out a black and white photo of a young woman. She set it in front of me.

The woman was straight-backed, with a haughty expression, a long neck, fine, wide-set eyes, thick dark hair.

'What's this about? Why are you showing me this?'

'It's your mother, David. Your biological mother.'

'My mother? But where has this come from all of a sudden? When was it...? You told me you didn't know what she looked like.'

'It would have created complications. I couldn't.'

'What complications? Is she still alive? Where is she now?'

'Honestly I don't know if she's—'

'What's her name, my mother?'

'Elena Pereyra.'

'Why did she give me up? Why didn't she keep me?'

'*Cariño*, I never had any contact with her, it was all done through third parties.'

'I don't get it. Why all this secrecy? Why couldn't you show me this years ago?'

'Because your father would never have forgiven me.' She ran her finger across the photograph, as if tracing the outline of the face. 'She was Jewish, David.'

'Jewish?'

Rocío had taken my hand, which I pulled away. 'Yes, darling. A Jew, a proper Jew, not a *conversa* or anything like that.'

I remember feeling an alarming sense of vertigo.

'I don't understand at all. She was a Jew? What does that make me? I'm Jewish, then. Am I? Or what?'

'No, darling, you are Catholic. You've been brought up a Catholic.'

After that, my mind was a whirl. All the moral values my adoptive parents had pummelled into me, all the stuff about church and family life and respect for authority and hierarchy, what did it mean now? They had a very conservative version of the faith; Vatican II cut no ice in our household. But this guff was theirs, not mine. Two starchy aliens who called themselves my parents and said they loved me but never hugged me or held my hand. Theirs, along with the gloomy over-decorated apartment, the stilted mealtimes, the porcelain, the carriage clocks and the boredom.

Except it *was* mine, whether I liked it or not. Catholicism was woven into my sense of self. I'd been brought up attending mass, confirmation classes, confession – I still remember, when I was about nine, racking my brains to come up with invented sins I could own up to. I donated pocket money for the poor of Equatorial Guinea, said prayers for the souls of godless Soviets. Got goosebumps at the sight of the faithful in their triangular hoods during the Holy Week processions…

I might reject it and fight against it, but at least I knew where I stood with it. It was part of me. And still is. Agonising over my personal responsibility for the loss of the Pandora and its crew, I've even said to Margalit, 'I need to redeem myself,' and she made a wry face and said, 'Redemption is such a *Christian* concept, darling.'

And even if I could wrench myself free of a Catholic upbringing, what then? A *Jew*? Hell! I had no notion at that time of what it meant to be a Jew. All I knew was that in my adoptive parents' world, Jews were on a par with gypsies. Not the Aguileras' kind at all, not *gente decente*. Itinerants, never putting down roots, couldn't be trusted to be faithful to the Fatherland. Jews, freemasons, communists: my parents' axis of evil. Who'd be a Jew, for Christ's sake!

When Rocío revealed the secret, I kept saying, 'You should have told me.'

'I'm sorry. We were only trying to protect you.'

'Protect me from what? Protect me from being a Jew?'

'It doesn't change anything, you know.'

'It changes everything! I'm not who I thought I was.'

'You are who you always were, darling. Yourself, just yourself.'

She put her hand on mine and withdrew it. 'I was so desperate for a baby, you can't imagine. The pain of trying for years and nothing happening. And your father not saying anything, but looking at me as if it was my fault. Eventually we gave up. Then out of the blue, you come along. Love at first sight, truly.' She'd smiled and dabbed her eyes. 'I'm so sorry if you feel I've not been a proper mother to you.'

I'd made apologetic noises. 'It's not that I…'

'I know.'

I said, 'I'd like to keep that photograph.'

'Of course, my love, it's yours.'

Later that afternoon, she'd been in tears again when I'd left and taken a taxi to the airport. *Elena*, I thought, *my mother's name is Elena* and it sent a shiver down my spine.

A few days later I wrote to Rocío, calmer and a little remorseful, to ask her to help me get in touch with my 'biological' mother.

10.

Meeting her, my 'real' mother, after all those years didn't go as I'd imagined. It was in 2005, over six months after Rafa had died and not long after I'd moved in with Margalit.

One of those fine early summer days in Madrid. Warm and fresh, before the punitive heat of July and August. The first time I'd set eyes on her since she gave me up for adoption. Elena Pereyra. I was as nervous as hell, like before a battle. Or a first date.

She was waiting for me in a café on the Castellana. Younger than I'd visualised her, too young to be my mother, surely. That made sense, though. She must have been still in her teens when she had me.

The shock of recognition was much stronger than when I'd seen the photograph from Rocío's box. That didn't get across her energy, her vitality in the flesh. Her eyes, chestnut brown, still bright, were like mine. I imagined they could be fiery, could narrow into a fearsome glare at the insolent or stupid. Her posture, the way she held her neck, was mine too. Or mine was hers. The thick wavy hair cut quite short and tucked behind her ears, with flecks of grey – it was like seeing myself, as a woman and nearly two decades older.

I wanted to embrace her, and I wanted to be angry with her. I just held out my hand. She got up, and there we were, standing on the brown and cream squares of the café's marble tile floor, like chess pieces that didn't know how they were supposed to move. She took my hand in both hers, looking at me. I'd intended to be brisk and businesslike, but when she suddenly flung her arms around me and pressed me to her, I had to clench to keep from breaking down in tears.

'My son, my son. Is it really you? I can't believe it.' She uttered a long-drawn-out cry, almost like a funeral wail, in the middle of the famous old café, unconcerned by the glances of the other customers.

'You were a tiny baby and now you're a man, a proper man! And so handsome!' She gave a great sob, and almost simultaneously a chuckle.

So handsome. That's what a mother is bound to say.

'I never thought this day would come. I can't believe it, I cannot believe it.'

I said, 'Perhaps this isn't the place to…'

But she was hugging me again, and I felt my heart thumping against her breast.

We sat, and ordered coffees and she looked at me, kept looking at me. I felt as if, standing on a wild shore, I'd been hit by a rushing wave that tumbled me off my feet, winded me, and at the same time left me tingling with exhilaration. I could only smile, and shake my head, and stutter meaningless beginnings before words dried up. 'I don't know... This is, I don't know... so strange.'

Of course, I still felt anger and bitterness at a mother who hadn't loved me enough to keep me, as I saw it. But something more, too. In this busy café, at the marble-topped table, across from this handsome middle-aged woman, there was a sense of slotting into my place in the world.

In the midst of the tears and the laughter, she sniffed and said, 'Sorry, it's just I can't bear the thought of all the things I've missed. It's been so long, it's felt like a lifetime.'

She asked me if I was married, if I had children.

'I have a partner. It's quite recent. And a step-daughter. We hope to have another child.'

'That's wonderful. I'd like to meet them.'

'I'm sure you will.'

'Well,' she said.

'Well,' I echoed, and there was an awkward pause. I said at last, smiling, 'So what do you do for a living, Elena?' It was a dumb question.

'I work for the city council. Like my father did. In housing and urban planning. Regeneration, that sort of thing. Madrid's changed in the last twenty or thirty years, you wouldn't believe. All those new developments, Las Rozas, Majadahonda, the M40.'

'Ah-ha,' I said. 'Interesting.'

She talked about her job, about having worked to put herself through college, getting a business studies diploma. I nodded, asked polite questions. Until there was another uncomfortable void waiting to be filled. Almost simultaneously, we lifted our coffee spoons, stirred our drinks, took sips, sighed: displacement activity. I shifted in my chair, looked around me; no one was paying us any attention.

'I know what you want to ask,' she said abruptly, looking me in the eyes. 'Why did I give you away? And why didn't I search for you?'

'Yes, of course. And you being Jewish. And me being Jewish – if I am. A Jewish Catholic, a Catholic Jew?'

'So much to say. I don't know where to begin, I want to hear all about you. Look at you, a grown man now! I can't believe it.'

I stroked her hand clumsily. 'You gave me away.' I'd tried to say it gently, but it came out brusque, a bit harsh.

'It wasn't like that.'

I wanted her to say, *yes, it was terrible, the worst mistake I ever made*. And then I wanted to go back in time and have her sit and hold me tight and soothe

78

me. Rocío and Rafael, who loved me in their own chilly manner, had so often left me alone to let my childish tantrums blow themselves out. I saw myself again as that small boy, curled up under the covers, gnawing at my knuckles till they bled, furious at some paternal reprimand or slight.

'I don't understand,' I said.

'I didn't really get what was happening. I was young and stupid. Would I have done the same if I had my time over? I hope not.'

'You still aren't sure you'd have kept me?'

'David, you sound hostile. I'm trying to be honest. I owe you that.'

'So why couldn't you keep me, Elena?'

She was silent for so long I wanted to nudge her.

'You have to imagine. Everything so prescribed and set out for me, I was in a straitjacket. Still a teenager and already my parents expecting me to marry a nice Jewish boy. They had one lined up, of course – Jacobo. He'd inherited a furniture whole-sale business in the calle Toledo. They all expected me to settle down, have kids; in other words, give them grandchildren, keep a kosher home. That was the plan. Their plan.'

'And you married him, this Jacobo?'

She nodded. 'Family pressure. Nice enough fellow, a bit dull, conventional. No imagination. Also quite controlling. And the worst thing...' She stopped and searched in her handbag, and shut it again. 'There was no... no real passion.' She laughed, and I shivered because it was like hearing myself laugh.

'I wanted to see the world,' she continued, 'learn languages, paint, work in bars, dance in all the sleazy nightclubs. After Franco, you know, you took the screws off and everyone went a bit crazy. Imagine, a naive, Bohemian Jewish girl in Madrid in the mid-seventies!'

'You'd rather see the world than care for your own son.'

'That was before...' she began. Then, 'David, you're angry, I get that. But please let me try to explain.'

'I'm sorry, it's difficult.'

'Yes.' She took a breath, composed herself. 'Met this guy at some reception I wasn't supposed to be at. Businessman, didn't know I was Jewish. Fabián. Thirty-five, maybe. Very charming, as long as you didn't get him onto politics. Or Jews. Also married, of course.'

'So you cheated on your husband.'

She gasped.

'I'm sorry,' I said. 'That was out of order.'

'Yes. Yes, I did. But look, David, we're all fallible humans, and I was young.'

It felt like a well-deserved reproach. I blushed. I'd so wanted to be calm and rational, keep things on an even keel. But I couldn't. 'I still don't understand why you couldn't just have been a mother to me.'

She took a breath. 'Things were complicated back then. Pressures. Social attitudes. You have to remember there was a whole culture of removing babies from single mothers, something that very much carried on after Franco. And I was just a girl.'

'But old enough to have a baby.'

She made a noise as if I'd punched her in the guts, an *oof*. 'I'm just trying to let you see things through my eyes.' She seemed suddenly fragile and unsure of herself, on the verge of tears. 'Please, David, it's so wonderful to... I don't want things to be bitter.'

After another silence, she said, 'I fell pregnant. Not Jacobo's. Everyone horrified. Parents threatening to disown me. Then they just ground me down. Ground me down. Practically stole you from me in the end, and I had nowhere to turn.'

'*Stole* me?'

'I was cornered, you know, I had no choices. Couldn't see any other way out. Except, you know...'

'What?'

She gave an apologetic half-smile. 'Do away with myself, I suppose.'

'Surely not.'

'Sounds dramatic, I know. I mean, I did consider it.' She gazed into space, towards the gilded mirror, with its reflection of the bar, the marbled tabletops, the white pillars. 'I scoped out the possibilities, even. I don't know, throw myself off that viaduct on the calle

81

Belén. Into the traffic. Or the Manzanares... But of course, I'd never have done it. I kept thinking, *what if I landed on a car?* I was a melodramatic teenager. Just happened to have a husband and was about to give birth to a baby that wasn't his. Anyway. It doesn't matter now, I want to hear about you and your life.'

I shuddered at the thought that I, not yet born, might have become collateral damage in a suicide attempt.

'How can you say it doesn't matter?' I said.

'I didn't mean it like that. Look, I survived, found a little flat, made a life, got a good job at the Ayuntamiento. Had relationships.'

I could hear Elena's voice, her words, but I couldn't take them in. They seemed to merge with the murmuring, echoing voices of the clientele in the café. Then I sensed the black cloud descending, without warning, like when I was a kid. That's what I named it to myself: the black cloud. A friendless, abandoned, un-nurtured feeling. A cloud that pressed down on you, seeped into you, stained things. Took the joy and meaning out of the world. No place of refuge. I sat silent for a few moments, overwhelmed by competing impulses. I felt myself doing what I'd learned to do in my adoptive childhood: retrench, put up the defences, survive the black cloud.

'What?' she said.

I stood up. The grating of the chair legs on the marble floor set my teeth on edge.

'What are you doing, David? Why are you getting up? Please sit down.'

'I'm sorry, Elena. It's me. I can't do this. I thought I could, but I'm not ready for it. It's too... I need time to process it all.'

'You can't go already. Please.' She reached out as if she was about to grasp my hand but stopped herself and brought her own hand awkwardly to her bosom.

'It's too much.'

She shook her head, trying not to cry. 'Will I see you again?'

'Yes, of course, I'd like to talk about being Jewish, sort of Jewish. Some other time. I mean, I don't know. I don't know, I'm sorry.'

I said a stiff and hurried goodbye, realising as I did so that she'd have loved to embrace me again, and I her. But I couldn't. I turned and made my way, my face taut, through the maze of close-packed tables towards the exit. As I walked out onto the boulevard with its sun-dappled lines of acacias and plane trees, I was on the verge of tears, devastated by my own fragility.

11.

I've come to see Elena today, which is why that difficult first meeting back in 2005 has been in my mind. She's been quite unwell lately. First time I've left the flat in days. Good to get out, but also disorienting, strange to be with other people on the metro, in the street. At sea I can go for months at a time without coming across a face I don't recognise, or an individual whose precise place in our little world I don't know.

Elena has sat me down in the kitchen of her small, airy apartment in Cuatro Caminos. She pours coffee and smiles, but she's moving slowly and her face is puffy.

'You know I've been having health problems.'

'Yes, since before I went away. How are you doing? How's the pain?'

'Well, you know they sent me for tests, I think I told you last time you were here. And they've all come back…'

'And?'

'So now they've told me I've got pancreatic cancer.'

'Hell, Elena! Cancer? How could that happen?'

'David, *cariño*, things happen. We've all got to die.'

I feel guilty I've only visited her a couple of times since returning from the Baltics. Too wrapped up in my own problems. I only came today because she messaged me asking me over for a coffee.

'But you're still young.'

'The specialist says it's the luck of the draw. No lifestyle or genetic factors. Random. Like crossing a minefield, just happened to step on one.'

'So what does that mean, I mean in terms of...'

'How long have I got? A few months. Maybe.'

'Christ, Elena.' I shake my head.

'If I get past my next birthday, I'll be reasonably satisfied. But, hey, they'll give me happy pills and potions, make me comfortable.'

She takes my hand and squeezes it. 'Don't get upset. Not for me. I'm okay, *hijo mío*. Relieved. I feel better now I know.'

'Rubén will be devastated. Don't know how I'm going to break it to him.'

He and she have built quite a relationship. She manages to bring him out of his shell, is his confidant about goings-on at school, or Sara's teasing. She gets him giggling merrily when she tries to play computer games with him and hams up her hopelessness.

'I can talk to him myself if you like. Kids are pretty resilient when it comes to these things.'

She offers me a brandy. I take a gulp. I keep saying, 'I'm so sorry, Elena,' as if it's my fault. 'Why didn't you tell me?'

'I didn't know. Now I do. So I've told you.'

I look at her in disbelief, denial.

'I've decided against chemo,' she says.

'Why on earth?'

'Because it's brutal, medieval.'

'But—'

'They'll look back in thirty, forty years and say, how could they subject people to that! And it's only postponing the inevitable.'

I'm thinking, *But what about me? Your son. I want you to 'postpone the inevitable', I want to have you around for longer.* I don't say it, of course.

'Don't look so glum,' she says.

We chat for a while, about the past; about our first, unhappy, meeting; about the kids. She's getting tired and asks me to help her into bed. She lies on her back, eyes closed, breathing laboured. Thinking she's gone to sleep, I'm heading for the door when she opens her eyes and says, 'Just come back here a moment.'

I return to her bedside.

'What's going on with you and Margalit?'

'What do you mean?'

'Don't think I don't know.'

I sigh.

'David, she's solid gold. You know that.'

'It's complicated. I'm going through a lot right now, with Margalit, with the inquiry – work stuff. And...' I stop.

'Oh, come on,' she says, 'don't make me cross.' The effort takes its toll, and she coughs. 'You're a commander, David, a leader of men, don't give me nonsense about difficulties and complications, just get on with it.'

I smile to myself because not many people would talk to me like that. I don't feel much like a leader of men these days. But I know she's right. I just don't know how to go about it.

I cannot believe my mother, barely sixty, has a terminal illness while that desiccated old Francoist woman across the road goes on and on. When I get back to the Chamberí flat, she's energetically scaring away the pigeons from her potted plants with a tea towel, like they're illegal immigrants. 'Shoo! Shoo!' she goes. The pigeons flap-flap away and disperse. They'll be wheeling back soon, no doubt. If I had an airgun, I'd want to take potshots, and not at the pigeons.

12.

The doorbell rings and for one deluded moment I think it might be Margalit returning. My heart bounds and I quickly clear the coffee table. But it's not her; when I pick up the intercom, I hear a familiar male voice.

'*No te hagás el boludo, che, abrí la puerta de una puta vez!*' Just open the fucking door, asshole.

Marce, channelling his inner Argentinian. I buzz him in.

We embrace. 'Get yourself a beer, Marce.'

'And one for you?'

'No thanks.'

He gives me his quizzical look and goes through to the kitchen.

Thank God I had Marce with me in the Baltics. He's my subordinate, of course. But also the brother I never had, friend, counsellor about the normal world. With me, he can say what he likes, though he knows to hold back, be diplomatic, when I'm *Captain*

Aguilera and he's *Lieutenant* Feigenbaum. He's one of the few people who dares tell me to my face that I've messed up. How, for example, when I'm stressed, I become more domineering and intolerant of dissent. Like when the Pandora was in trouble and I prowled around biting out acerbic orders to scurrying crew members, raising my voice to laggards. Marce took me aside and murmured in my ear, 'Easy, *mi capitán*, you have them well-drilled, they all know exactly what to do.' Before I could snap back, he'd gone, and I realised he was right.

That authoritarian streak reflects, I suppose, the unconscious influence of my adoptive father. Which is ironic. I vividly remember an incident from when I was still in infant school, I must have been about five. I come out of my bedroom one evening before dinner to find my father pacing the living room, clasping and unclasping his hands and breathing heavily. The television is on much louder than usual, my mother is trying to persuade him to sit down and have a camomile tea.

'Camomile tea! No, Rocío, woman, I don't need something to calm me down, for crying out loud. A brandy or something! Get me a brandy, a large one.'

A brandy, a large one – that always meant it was a special occasion.

Rafa goes and stands in front of the television clenching his fist, shouting, 'Yes! Yes!' like he's at a football match.

'What's the matter with *papi*?' I ask my mother.

'Nothing. Go to your room.'

'No, woman!' says my father. 'Let him stay, this is history in the making.'

There's a large hall, curved rows of seats getting higher towards the back, men and women sitting around looking scared. At the front, on a sort of platform, a man in the uniform of a policeman, a *guardia civil*. He's holding a pistol, tiny in his massive hand. His shiny black hat has funny wings to each side, and I really want one the same. He's got an enormous moustache, like an upside-down V. He shoots his pistol at the ceiling, and shouts, 'On the floor! On the floor!'

'Is it a film, *papi*?'

'No, it's real. It's happening right now. He's a lieutenant colonel!' my father shouts, pointing at the man with the big moustache. 'You see the stars on his sleeve? You could be a lieutenant colonel one day!'

Some other civil guards come in with proper big guns, and push people around and shout at them. 'What's going on, *papi*?'

'Spain is getting its honour back!'

His eyes look a bit mad. 'I don't understand. What do you mean? What are those men doing?'

A sudden burst of gunfire startles me. I say, 'I think I'll go to bed now.'

'No, you won't, you'll stay here and watch.' My father laughs and – unusually for him – puts his arm around me. He says, 'Courage, boy, this is no time to be afraid.'

The television is showing the outside of a big white building with columns, and voices are saying they hope to have the pictures back soon. 'The Congress of Deputies – parliament,' my father says with scorn, making me think 'parliament' is a bad thing.

Later, I was sent to bed, but I could still hear the announcers on the TV, and Rafa laughing, and talking to himself. 'What a pair of balls on him! *Arriba España, arriba, coño!*' Then I heard him on the phone, banging his fist and swearing a lot and talking very loudly. Lots of important-sounding music playing.

Do I really remember all this? I've seen the television footage of that day so many times since. And I've heard my father retelling the events, with bitterness for what might have been. One of the few times he expressed deep emotion about anything. The day after, the king made a speech and Tejero's attempted coup collapsed. My father slumped in his armchair when he heard the news, muttering to himself, 'It can't be, it can't be.' My mother hustled me, confused and sleepy, off to school, although perhaps that was the next day or later, because they closed the schools for a while. I had a notion something very serious was happening, but couldn't grasp what it was.

These days, a part of me thinks that maybe my father was right, at some level. Loosen the reins and soon everybody's at each other's throats. Whether it's a family or a country. Or now Europe, fragmenting, divided against itself, in economic meltdown, conflicts breaking out all along its borders. But the last thing you'd want is another Franco. So any autocratic impulses that (according to Marce at least) I might have, I sternly suppress. Or try to.

As an adviser, Marce is often spot on, both on military and personal matters. He'd make his pertinent (and often impertinent) observations even while we were trekking across country in the Baltics, trying to stay away from Russian patrols and trigger-happy militias. We kept to the country roads or hiked over fields, heading north. Untilled land, ragwort spreading across pastures, reeds choking the streams: signs of breakdown everywhere. We'd bed down for the night in gloomy abandoned barns, and get up hungry and damp, and hike through the drizzle until we were exhausted. Always, Marce buoyed me up, kept me going. My gadfly, court jester.

Once, early on, we woke up in this barn, nestled close for warmth, still stiff with cold. Marce props his head up on one hand.

'I can understand why a man might want to be faithful while his kids are vulnerable. There's an evolutionary logic to it. But once they're old enough to fend for themselves, there's no biological imperative. Faithfulness becomes just a social institution designed to keep women happy while men are miserable.'

'I'm not sure what Stone Age cave you crawled out from,' I say, 'but—'

'I mean the word itself. *Faithfulness*. All those religious connotations. *The Faith. The faithful*. You've only got to watch any crappy American TV drama to see how deeply rooted it is in their psyche.' He puts on a high falsetto. '"Darling, you've been unfaithful to me, it's over between us." It's the Protestant ethic, the Puritans, Thanksgiving, turkeys and all that.'

And the Catholic ethic, I think. His insistent voice is comforting in a funny way, like muzak.

'Cue bitter tears,' he says, 'acrimonious divorce proceedings and an eye-watering financial settlement. And all because he stuck his *pirulín* in some *mina's*—'

'So where's this going?'

'These people do not understand the human condition.'

'Whatever you say, Marce.'

He looks at me, slyly. I know that look. It means he's leading up to something. 'All the evidence points to it.'

'What evidence? I'm cold and hungry. Just get to the damned point.'

'Oh, you know. The furrowed brow. The reverence with which you talk about Margalit.'

'What have I got to do with your ramblings?'

'The smell of some woman's soap on you when we met up on the ferry? That unfeasibly huge hunk of salami? All pointing to you having shagged some local *mina, che*!'

He's right, and he's wrong. I think back to Kamilė, who saved me when I had an infected wound, with her handsome face, wide cheekbones, sad grey eyes. The whiff of something like cinnamon or cedar wood on her skin. Kamilė with whom nothing happened. But only because I left her cottage before it did.

I smile at my friend. 'As a point of fact, you're wrong. And don't project your libidinous urges onto me.'

Marce chuckles. 'And of course, you muttering something or other in your sleep.'

'Muttering what?'

'While trying to spoon me, or take me from behind, or whatever you were doing.'

'Nonsense. Abstinence has addled your brain.' I turn and pat my comrade on the side of the neck, as if to say, 'There, there.'

'So a dark horse, eh, *mi capitán*?'

'Shut the hell up, Lieutenant, it's time we made a move.'

I smile at the memory, while feeling yet another pang of guilt, that I'd betrayed Margalit in my

heart, if not with my body. Things had been difficult between us since well before I left for the Baltic.
Because of my self-absorbed bitterness about being
posted there in the first place when I'd been set for
a stellar career. My tendency to brood, to not be all
there, to spend my shore leave thinking about the
next mission. My continuing failure to work out
what being a Jew meant for me, if anything at all.

13.

Marce has got himself a beer from my fridge and paces around the living room, picking up items at random and examining them, replacing them any old how. He takes a card from the bookshelves.

'*Los Sefardíes en el mundo*,' he reads. 'Margalit Toledano. Blah blah. Her book launch? So it's out at last?'

'Let me see that.' I take the card from his hand. How come I haven't noticed it before? Perhaps Sara left it when she popped in the other day. And why hasn't Margalit said anything to me? Or perhaps she has, and I've been too wrapped up in myself to register it.

'Respect to her!' Marce says. '*Mazeltov.* Getting a book published, that's some achievement after all these years. What with two kids plus you to look after.'

I make a mental note of the date of the launch and slip the card into an enamelled pot of odds and ends on a shelf.

Marce looks out of our French windows, waves at the disapproving old lady opposite who's sweeping her balcony, comes and sits down.

'So,' he says, 'what gives, *compadre*? What's good and new?'

'Just been to see my mother, Elena. She's not in a great state.'

'Oh? I'm sorry to hear that, David.'

'It seems to be terminal.'

'God, that's shitty news.' He leans forward, rubs my upper arm. 'I'm so sorry.'

We sit in silence for a while. He shakes his head, trying to take it in. He's met Elena a few times and really warmed to her.

'So how're you doing?'

I shrug.

'Let me know if you want to talk.'

'Thanks.'

'Are you keeping yourself busy?'

'Apart from worrying about my mother, I'm just sitting here, waiting. Waiting for the inquiry. Like you, I imagine.'

'I'm not just sitting around. I'm out there, doing things.'

He narrows his eyes, sniffs the air.

'And Margalit?'

'How d'you mean?'

'The state of the place, I mean... There's an absence here.'

'Margalit's taken a few days respite care.'

'From you?'

'At least, she said a few days. Maybe more.'

'What the hell! And you expected *her* to move out?'

'She just packed and left.'

'Oh, she just packed and left, did she? Why didn't you say, "You stay, you've got the kids, I'll find somewhere"? Christ's sake.'

'I don't have anywhere else.'

'There's a spare room at my place, you're welcome to it. I'm about the only one who could put up with you, and we could work on our evidence for the inquiry together.'

'I don't think so. It'll look like I'm taking a step further away from her.'

'You've always had space, the pair of you, because you've always been at sea for long periods. It was never going to help work out your problems, you being stuck here getting under her feet in the flat for weeks on end.'

'I'll think about it.'

'Ten days, maybe. Doesn't have to be for long, she'll want you back. And I won't want you there forever, *pelotudo de mierda*, cramping my style.

Nice modern flat, Las Delicias. Three bedrooms. Oh, and one other lodger. Laura.'

'Laura your ex-wife Laura?'

'Yes, that Laura. Ex, but we're on amicable terms.'

'Oh yeah,' I say, knowingly.

As he leaves, Marce pats me on the back and says, 'The flat, think about it.'

I'm thinking about it. Maybe it'd be good for me to go to Marce's for a week or two, unpick the problems. I phone Margalit, put it to her that she comes back here with the kids. She sounds wary at first, as if it's a trap of some kind. When she realises it's not, she's delighted. 'That would make life a lot easier. So yes.'

'We'll talk,' I say.

'If and when you're ready to talk, David, we'll talk.'

14.

One bone of contention has been that Margalit thinks I could be a better father, though she knows I do try. I don't like to say it to her, but it's partly about having a daughter who isn't my 'real' daughter. I know Sara comes with Margalit, is part of the package, but still. Also, I've been so on edge since the Baltics. Margalit thinks that's not a good reason to take things out on the kids, and that I don't make allowances for the fact that children invariably generate chaos.

Like what happened a few weeks ago over the Friday evening meal. Everything set out for the Shabbat. Rubencito grabs a slice of cold beef. Sara shouts at him. He grabs another with his fingers, and takes a bite out of each slice, making mocking noises. I say, 'Stop it, the pair of you.' Sara has a pop-eyed glare – maybe she learned it from me. She says, 'Put one back, you moron!' Margalit goes, 'Kids, please, it's Shabbat!' Rubén eats his meat with lip-smacking noises, *mmm-mmm-mmm*, looking at Sara, trying to provoke her. She goes, 'Pathetic specimen!' in that sneering adolescent voice she does so well, and lunges across the table and hits him. He yelps. 'Ow, my arm! She punched me!' As Sara sits down, her arm catches the Shabbat candle, knocks it over, hot wax all over the white tablecloth.

I stand up and bellow, 'Enough!' The voice of authority. Could quell an onboard mutiny. Maybe overkill for fractious kids. Margalit's watching me disapprovingly. Sarita is shocked into silence. They hate when I lose it.

'Rooms!'

'David,' murmurs Margalit, 'it's Shabbat.'

The kids get down, both near tears now, while Margalit clears up the mess on the table, lips tight. When they've both left the dining room, I say, 'And you think they're starting to get on?'

'David, they're kids. Kids squabble. And he did provoke her.'

'Kids? Sara's a teenager and Rubén's in his bar mitzvah year, as you keep telling me. What a performance.'

She stops her cleaning and turns to me. 'Darling, do you think you could possibly under-react once in a while?'

I stare at her.

'Sometimes I think they behave like that to get a rise out of you.'

'They might behave better if we didn't indulge them.'

I regret using that tone. But apologising isn't my strong suit. I guess that's part of the problem.

I lay in bed that night, fretting over my outburst, wondering why it was all so difficult. I'd never have got away with such behaviour as a child. Rafa used to say, 'Spain is a family, a good Catholic family, and democracy is destroying it. Look at these politicians, all they do is squabble with each other then take their cut.' Maybe, as much as I rejected my upbringing, I still have a fair slice of Rafa in me.

A couple of days later, Margalit said, 'You know, David, sometimes when people try to treat a problem, the act of intervening stirs things up. Like prodding a wasp's nest. But people, especially men, don't like it when you say, "Leave well alone, don't do anything".'

I rose to the bait. 'By "especially men", darling, you mean me?'

'Take it however you like.' She cocked her head and gave me a wry look.

I hate the idea that there's nothing to be done.

But I retain that image of myself, with a long stick, prodding away at a wasp's nest.

15.

My mobile goes. It's van Raalte, wanting a chat. I hardly have the excuse that I'm too busy to talk to him. I press answer. There he is, with his square head and his shiny brow at the bottom of the screen, as if I'm supposed to address the light bulb directly above him rather than the man himself. He wants to walk me through aspects of my career; if only, he says, because it will come up at the Pandora sinking inquiry.

'In 2013, you were appointed commander of a frigate?' His Spanish accent is appalling, the rhythm's all wrong, and he insists on using the formal *usted* manner of address, which practically nobody in Madrid does any more. But his Spanish is better than my English, so Spanish it is.

'Correct. The Galene. In the Aegean.'

'And in 2014 you were relieved of command of the Galene.'

'Correct.'

'Can you explain why?'

'How long have you got, *Licenciado*?'

My glorious career hit a brick wall. Margalit would say I shouldn't go on about it, but it left a bitter taste. The episode was why I ended up policing Baltic herring in a rickety patrol boat.

'Basically,' I say, 'it was EuDeFor politics. The Italians were pushing for more Italian commanders, and I was collateral damage.'

'We can't use that, obviously. Wasn't there a refugee problem?'

'There was, but our task was impossible. Or contradictory. We were supposed to protect terrified migrants plus guarantee the integrity of marine frontiers. Which meant turning desperate refugees back in unseaworthy boats. You can do one or the other, not both.'

'So are you saying you had no responsibility for what happened?'

'No. Of course I had responsibility. But they put me in an impossible position. I did the best I could – pick up survivors of capsized boats, take them to ports in Greece or Cyprus or Italy. Turn into a hate figure for the local mad-eyed zealots. I mean, I tried.'

'You tried?'

'For instance, ignored orders not to pick up refugees from a boat sinking off the coast of Turkey. Even took off my headset and told the area controlling officer, *You're breaking up, sorry, can't hear you.* Obviously we can't use that at the inquiry.'

'No indeed,' says van Raalte. 'Even though you were arguably acting in accordance with the laws of the sea. Article 98 of the UN Convention.'

'Very possibly. But it won't cut much ice with the EuDeFor panel.'

'That is true.'

'So the trouble starts when I pick up a consignment of refugees and head to the nearest port. Mavrolimni, it was called. Didn't realise it was a snake pit. The militias controlled the local authorities, the police. Ended up having to leave the male refugees to their fate and then go on to Piraeus to offload the women and children. Turns out some of the men left behind were massacred. I'd wanted to shell the militia positions in the hills but EuDeFor vetoed it.'

'And you were suspended. For disobeying orders?'

'Or for not disobeying orders. Who knows. For failing to protect the refugees when EuDeFor made it impossible for me to do so.'

'You were cleared by the official inquiry, which was critical of the naval hierarchy for confusion and unclear or unworkable directives.'

'Yes. Much good did it do me. My command wasn't restored, for "operational reasons" or some bullshit. Though my frigate commander's salary was protected. My lawyer at the time said I should be thankful for the outcome, that an appeal would be counterproductive.'

'You were badly advised.'

'Thanks for telling me.'

Van Raalte's bespectacled, sweating head sinks even further down the screen in response to my sarcasm.

'Anyway,' I say, 'that's how I came to be relocated to the Baltic Sea.'

'As captain of the Pandora?'

'Correct. And EuDeFor thought I should be duly grateful to be in charge of a patrol vessel that should have long since been decommissioned, with sonar so obsolete you couldn't tell your herring shoals from your jellyfish swarms.'

Just talking about it brings back those smells of old naval boat that got to me the first time I went aboard the Pandora: the acrid piss smell of rusting steel, pervasive diesel fumes, sour human sweat below decks, the whiff of rancid, reused cooking oil when you got near the galley. So unlike the fresh, bristling, businesslike aromas of my Aegean frigate.

'Hmm,' says van Raalte, enigmatically, and he takes off his glasses to wipe them on a paper tissue.

'What?'

'That's helpful.'

I doubt it. He ends the call.

Back in 2015, when I told Margalit about the Baltic assignment, she said, 'I don't even know what use you are, sailing up and down the Baltic. The state we're in, you'd think they could find better use for their resources.'

'I'm lucky to have a posting.'

I think she was more disappointed than she'd admit that my career had stalled when it had all seemed so promising. I used to track the troubles in our marriage back to that point, but I know it's about more than that.

'It's not me who arranges these things, *cariño*.' I thought sourly of the mission, putting an end to over-fishing of Baltic herring. 'Everything's connected. What happens there affects us, it affects the whole of Europe. The same way events in Germany affected Jews two thousand kilometres away in Salonica, you should know that.'

'What, even herring?' Margalit said. 'Will we be having herring wars?'

'We've had cod wars and shellfish skirmishes, so I guess it's on the cards.'

'Rubén won't be happy. Maybe you can explain it to him yourself.'

'And Sara?'

'She's staying with her father this weekend. And his boyfriend. She says things to me like, "I think I might be bisexual".'

'Really? Is it a phase?'

'It'll be what it'll be. But I don't suppose our *problemillas* help very much.' She sighed. 'But, you know what, I'm pleased for you, David. At least it's a step forward, isn't it?'

I didn't answer. It felt like a step along a career cul-de-sac.

I made the best of it. Along with the bad smells, the bad atmosphere assailed me as soon as I stepped aboard the Pandora. The former I could do little about. The latter I had to take rapidly in hand. The previous captain had retired, a popular man, but it's easy to be popular when you don't run a tight ship. The crew looked at me with a combination of resentment, hostility and – they knew my back story – pity. Pity was worst. You can't command a vessel if you're pitiable. It took a few months, but I had a strategy and stuck to it: winning over the waverers, isolating and crushing the few real trouble-makers. Being competent and effective, setting clear objectives. Getting the right people in the right positions: the Polish sonar operator, for example, with an uncanny knack for locating herring shoals and tracking them, or the young Spanish woman with a genius for maintaining ageing machinery when EuDeFor would not (sadly, the rudder and the back-up steerage were way beyond her pay grade). I made sure they knew I valued them for their contribution, and they responded. Every few days, I had a ritual exchange with Marce. 'How am I doing, Lieutenant?' 'Things are proceeding well, *mi capitán*.' Sardonic grin.

There was one refractory character whose bullying of younger, more junior crew and harassing of women had been tolerated and normalised under the previous regime. I challenged him. He had the most insolent sneer I've ever come across. I imposed the minor administrative sanctions available to me, loading him with extra work details, supervised drills, physical training. His little group of hangers-on quickly melted away when they realised I was serious, and eventually I had him put ashore in Karlskrona where he was arrested by EuDeFor military police to face more serious charges. After that, I had no problems with the crew, and we had an orderly, not to say harmonious, ship. I felt a sense of pride. On a smallish scale, I'd achieved something through my leadership. And then came the storm and the sinking.

16.

I'm getting a backpack of clothes and toiletries together to take to Marce's. I've decided it's the best thing to do. Going through my stuff, I've come across a plastic bag of items at the bottom of one of the cupboards. It was to have been donated to the synagogue's sale on behalf of members of the community suffering from 'fuel poverty', but must have been overlooked. I open it on impulse. Inside is a pullover I used to wear in my school days. Doubt it still fits me. Vertical stripes in blue and black, narrower ones in green, smelling of mothballs. Instantly I'm back in my teenage years.

Ash Wednesday, early nineties. We followed our teacher through the chilly streets to mass at the local church, took our seats in the pews. The priest was a little man in glasses, with a ridiculous strand of hair plastered across his head. He was going on about the blood and body of Christ, holding up the wine and the wafer.

Something about the coloured light through the stained-glass windows, the incense, the brightness of the candles in the gloom, put me in a heightened state. Not religious ecstasy, more the reverse: disenchantment, having a spell broken. The objects the priest was waving around weren't the blood and body of Christ, but everyday items. Probably bought at the local corner shop.

And I'd just had enough of the ritual. All the mumbo-jumbo about sin, repentance, imperfection of man, transience of our life on earth, sanctity of whatever. The not-to-be-questioned authority of the Church. The priest with his robes and his incantations and his horrible comb-over. I had a sudden feeling I was trapped in this weird other dimension, and I wanted to get out.

I joined the students lining up to be marked with the ash cross, got to the front of the queue. The priest had to reach up to make the sign in ash on my forehead, intoning, '*You are dust and to dust you shall return.*' Thanks, man. '*Repent and believe in the Gospel.*' I felt the anger rising. I looked down at the priest, rubbed the ash off my forehead, wiped it on my jumper – the one with the stripes – and told him, 'This is all nonsense.'

The priest looked like I'd threatened to knife him. I was fourteen, but already tall and stocky for my age. The teacher scurried over. 'Go to the back of the queue! You'll do it again and you'll do it properly.' I snorted with scorn, just stood there. The teacher muttered, 'Intolerable! You'll be hearing more about this.' He called to the queue of students, waving his hand crossly, 'Next! Next!' I walked out of the church, and nobody stopped me.

Of course, the school reported my little performance to my parents. My father summoned me to his study. 'What in God's name,' he rasped, 'is this outrageous behaviour! You've dishonoured a solemn day. Shamed your father.' Blah-blah-blah. 'Explain yourself!' I fixed my gaze on his desk, trying to block out his growling voice, not saying a word. In pride of place was a black-and-white photo in a silver frame, showing General Franco, aged and tubby with his dangling dewlaps like a tortoise, inspecting a line of officers that included a young Rafael Aguilera.

When Rafa had calmed a little, he interrogated me on what godless ideas had got into me and who was responsible. Did I have communist teachers or classmates? Or perhaps I'd been in contact with *curas rojos*, red priests, in which case, I was required to denounce them. I met his eyes and said, 'We live in a democracy these days, thank goodness, not in your rotten Francoist dictatorship.' Then, for the first and only time, he hit me. Not a punch, but a hard slap in the face. I put my fingers to the spot and laughed. Contemptuously – more of a snigger. 'Is that all you've got?' He sent me to my room with the stand-ard, 'You are punished.' This was his catchphrase when I'd committed some misdemeanour or other, uttered in a voice as clipped as his moustache – I'd always had the feeling I ought to click my heels and salute before complying. 'Gladly,' I said. I left him pacing up and down, muttering to himself.

Looking back, that Ash Wednesday drama was the moment I realised my father's power over me was limited and that if I chose to challenge or ignore him and his autocratic ways, there was only so much he could do about it.

It's taken me a long time, with much prodding (the 'wasp's nest' again?) from Margalit, to come to terms with my upbringing. I feel so unlike my adoptive parents, but so shaped by them. My father, Don Rafael as everyone called him, reached the rank of lieutenant colonel in an armoured infantry regiment under Franco. For him, Spain was Franco, Franco was Spain. The army was one of the great pillars of the regime, so he, Rafa, mattered. When Franco died, the champagne corks popped – which I don't remember, of course, it was before I was born – but Rafa ranted on about it often enough when I was growing up. Communists allowed back in from the cold! Socialists in power! Divorce, birth control, abortion legalised! 'Total lack of respect. Cut their damned balls off, that will teach them the virtues of abstinence.' He drifted towards embittered retirement, stuck in a desk job. I think he lived through me, vicariously. He wanted me to follow in his footsteps and join the army, ideally his old regiment.

So I applied to be a sailor.

'What,' said Margalit, 'a teenage revolt against your father?'

'Yes, I know, but it was a big thing for me at the time, and he hated it.'

'Mission accomplished?'

'I suppose so. He hated that I didn't provide him with a second-generation Lieutenant-Colonel Aguilera.'

He was a martinet. But, as Margalit made me see, he was still my father, and I suppose he loved me in his gruff, undemonstrative way. A difficult love, though.

I'd finished my EuDeFor basic training and was doing pretty well for myself as a junior officer in the North Atlantic fleet when I got a phone call from my adoptive mother: my father was in a bad way and I should come back to Madrid as soon as I could get compassionate leave. A few days later I flew home.

Rafael was lying in his hospital bed breathing through an oxygen mask. He lifted the mask and the first thing he said was not, 'Hello, David, hello my beautiful son,' but, 'It would have been so much easier if you'd been based in Madrid. Think about your poor mother.'

'I'm here now,' I said.

He coughed phlegm into a tissue. 'How's the boat?'

'It's a ship, *papá*, a battleship.'

'Well in that case,' he said, 'I suppose you're the last monkey.'

'I'm second lieutenant responsible for—'

'Yes, I'm sure, very good.' He wheezed and clutched at his oxygen mask.

'Shall I call a nurse?'

He waved the idea away.

'How do you feel?' I said, stupidly.

'I'm dying, how do you expect me to feel?'

I thought about taking his hand but couldn't do it.

He said, 'Dying. And disappointed.'

He made a tired, sweeping gesture with his arm that took in the view of Madrid from the window; the hospital room; me, the disappointing son.

He spluttered again. I thought he was exaggerating to make me feel guilty. I sat on the hard plastic chair, listening to the ticking of the machinery.

I finish packing my bag to take to Marce's. I suspect Margalit may already be imagining a life in which we're no longer together. Now, by going to Marce's, even for a couple of weeks, am I doing the same? In the circumstances, though, I don't see what else I can do. I don't like the idea at all. Perhaps that's why I'm taking the bare minimum with me.

17.

The news about Elena's health is nagging away at me as I travel from Chamberí to Marce's place in Delicias with my backpack. How strange it must be for her, now that her prospects are so short-term, so finite. It seems such a very long time since that first meeting. A world away. Afterwards, we spoke a few times on the phone, awkward edgy conversations. She was like an uncomfortable shadowy presence in my life, on the margins but hard to file away and forget about.

It was only when Rubén was a few weeks old, back in 2007, that I felt able to see her again. We met at the Botanical Gardens. The sandy paths were near-deserted, and we found a secluded bench in the shade.

'No baby?' Elena said.

'Next time. In the flesh, I promise.'

She'd been delighted when I'd phoned and told her I was now a father. It was something tangible to connect me to her. To show her I'd carried on the family line, I suppose.

Now she sat and scrolled through photos on my phone of Rubencito beaming in his mother's arms. A couple of me too, proud father.

'So gorgeous. He has your eyes, no?'

'I like to think so. And my *mal carácter*.'

'I doubt that.' She chuckled. 'Wonderful, wonderful! So I'm a grandmother. Amazing.'

'Yes,' I echoed, 'You're a grandmother. Rubén's grandmother.'

She threw her arms round me and kissed me. 'I have a grandson. Incredible.' Her joy gave way to pain. 'I'm so thrilled you did get back in touch. You can't imagine how I felt last time. When you walked out like that. I thought I might not see you again.'

I avoided her gaze, reaching instinctively for a cigarette I didn't have.

'I'm sorry,' I said. 'It was all too much. After so long. And the feeling that... You know. I'm away at sea a lot, I've been meaning to ring...'

I'd prepared what I was going to say, but when it came to it, I couldn't put words together. I knew only that I mustn't close up again, put on the armour plating.

'Please let him be in my life, at least a little,' she said.

'I'd love that.'

Her eyes lingered on me. 'I can't believe it, you have a son. My God! You change his nappies, and everything?'

'I do. When I'm home, obviously. I'd like to do more but I'm away a lot, and, you know...'

'Uh-huh.' She looked at me quizzically.

We sat and talked, variations on the theme of my being a grown man and a father, and then we'd smile without saying anything.

She shook her head and touched my arm, as if to make sure I was real, took a deep breath and sat very still. The sun was coming through the canopy of leaves, their shadows dancing in the gentle breeze. Birdsong.

'Am I like him, my father?'

'I don't know.' She laughed.

'No, but seriously, I mean…'

'Physically you are. But more like me.' She stroked me again. 'David, *cariño*, I think you're very like me.'

'Is he still alive, Fabián?'

'I lost touch with him years ago. In any case, he never laid eyes on you, never held you. Didn't want any responsibility for you.'

'So tell, me, Elena, this… thing with this man, with Fabián, how did you manage to…?'

'What, juggle it with my marriage? With difficulty. But you don't want to hear the whole story.'

'I do, though.' I was thinking, it might be sordid, but it's where I come from, my history. 'And,' I added, 'I promise I won't run off this time.'

She looked bitter for a moment, but her face cleared. 'Of course, I thought I was in love with him. Grown-up affair, posh hotel rooms, very hush-hush, exciting, no? In between rushing home to cook for Jacobo, and going to synagogue on Saturdays, I was like Fabián's kept woman. Sounds crazy, looking back. *Was* crazy. My parents nearly died of shame when they found out. Which is when I slink back home, after four months with Fabián, and say, hi *mami*, hi *papi*, I'm pregnant. And no, I can't marry him 'cos I've just got married, as you know, to Jacobo! And in fact, he's married too. Oh and by the way, he's not Jewish, and anyway he doesn't want to have anything more to do with me.'

Elena started crying, going, 'Oh dear, oh dear, I'm sorry,' and then embracing me and burying her face in my neck. I could feel her warm tears on my skin.

'If only you could have kept me,' I said softly. I wanted to say '*mamá*'.

'I know…' She put one hand to her chest. 'It was so difficult. I turned out not to be as brave and independent as I thought. My father refused to see me or speak to me, went round telling people he didn't have a daughter. After us having been so close. My husband said he wasn't going to help support the baby. "Under Jewish law, it's a *mamzer*. A *mamzer*, that's all there is to it."'

'A what?' I asked.

'A *mamzer*. It means bastard. A second-class citizen, can't take part properly in Jewish life. I was a married woman, remember, committing adultery. If the parents can't marry even in theory, the child's a *mamzer*. Back then, the community was intolerant about those things. Now, it's more "don't ask, don't tell".'

It made me think about the way the community had treated Margalit after she left Arturo and got together with me.

'The atmosphere when it all happened, you can't imagine. My dad too shocked and angry to talk to me, my mum in bits. Anyway, I went to the synagogue and spoke to the *mohel* – the man who does ritual circumcisions. He was horrible to me, Jacobo had told him everything. He wouldn't do it in synagogue. So I had to take you and get it done on a kitchen table at his house.'

I winced. It brought back the tough time I'd had at the naval barracks for being circumcised. My adoptive mother had always told me in a whisper, as if the neighbours might be listening, that as a child I'd had a *'problemilla médico'* that needed to be corrected.

'The circumcision didn't make any difference to Jacobo,' Elena continued. 'His attitude was, "a circumcised *mamzer* is still a *mamzer*." And he was being pressurised by his family. They launched a whole campaign, that I shouldn't keep the baby, that if I did he'd chuck me out on the street. They persuaded my parents it was for the best, and I felt isolated. They ground me down until I gave in. You were four weeks old and I loved you so, so much. But I had to agree to give you up for adoption. Not long after that, Jacobo announces he's leaving me anyway.'

The sudden anguish in her voice made it seem she was reliving the experience as if it had happened the day before, not three decades previously. 'So I'm completely on my own. No husband, no home. No baby.' She shivered, and wiped her eyes with the back of her hand.

I put my arm round her shoulder and rubbed her back. She calmed, and we sat close.

'Couldn't you have just said it was your husband's baby?'

'Yes, I could've tried. But I hadn't had sex with him for months. I told you, Jacobo wasn't very passionate. He was really only interested in money.' She smiled through her tears. 'Don't look so shocked, *cariño*. I couldn't bear it if you treated me like they all did.'

I pulled her against me, holding her tight and letting her weep, murmuring, 'It's okay, *mamá*, it's okay, it's okay.' I only let her go when there was the sound of footsteps on the path, and I sat leaning forward with my hands dangling between my knees.

'And how come I ended up with the Aguileras?' I said. 'With Catholic military people?'

'It's funny how these things happen.' She sounded calm again, remembering the distant past, not reliving it. 'When I told Fabián, my lover, I was expecting his child, his first reaction was, "Nonsense, girl. How do you know it's mine? How do I know it's not your husband's?" So I told him what I've just told you. He was flabbergasted. Mainly by the fact that my husband didn't have sex with me in six months. He thinks about it and then he says, "Well in that case, how do I know you haven't been sleeping around?"'

'Charming. So he washes his hands of the whole business? What about paternity tests and the like?'

'Maybe that's what he was afraid of, I don't know. Because suddenly he got back in touch to say he'd help with adoption. His wife's cousin was childless and looking to adopt a baby. Fabián organised everything through a Catholic priest, which was how things were done, and they took you, and I cried for a week solid. Like having my heart ripped out.' Her mouth twitched as though she was going to weep again. 'The priest gave me an envelope from Fabián with money in it.'

Elena's expression had grown dark. Eyes set, mouth hard.

'Money?' I said.

'Yes. Money. Banknotes. I threw it back at him and screamed I wanted my baby. But it was too late. Of course, my parents were happy to get you out of their sight, out of the Jewish community where you'd only be a reminder of the shame.' She smiled. 'But look, that's the story, there's no going back.'

I felt it made a kind of sense. I trusted her. What she'd told me was the pure truth.

'Now,' she said, 'I want to know more about you, more about your life. And then we can talk about when I get to see my grandson.'

So I did begin to tell her. I felt a bit stiff and reserved. Told her about how I'd followed my father's footsteps into the military. She gently got me to open up about how sombre my childhood had been. 'Was brought up a good Catholic. Was an altar boy, could have been a priest. That would have been ironic.'

'It wouldn't have mattered to me, you know, whatever you did.'

'Then I ended up in the navy. We're very inbred; it's a tight little world, the armed forces. We see civilians as an alien species. I feel at home on the ocean, and clumsy on dry land. Like a seal or something. But the navy saved me in a way. And Margalit, of course, she's been... Given me a sense of who I am, you know.'

I felt shocked by my frankness with her, this so familiar stranger. I'd only really talked about these things with Margalit.

'I understand.' She smiled. 'You're still so young, David. I think you'll be fine.'

'Young? If early thirties is young.'

'Young enough. And when am I going to meet Margalit and my grandson?'

'Soon. We'll figure something out.'

The light was fading, and the breeze was stiffening. She took my hand and rubbed it, and we sat there for a long time, shoulders touching, a weight lifted for both of us, until a bell sounded far off to warn visitors that the gardens were closing. We stood and headed for the exit, Elena threading her arm through mine.

18.

Marce is there to greet me when I arrive at his flat. I feel ill at ease, like I'm intruding, even though I know he's laid-back about me staying. 'Make yourself at home, *macho*,' he says. 'There's beer in the fridge and food at the corner shop.'

I suspect there'll be a leftover Marce stew in the fridge too, garlic skins and all. He looks at my small backpack of belongings. 'That all you've got?'

'Yes,' I say. 'I don't plan to stay long.'

The flat is modern and functional. He's contrived to make it look chaotic, with piles of his stuff still not unpacked lying in the hall, a bag of washing to be hung out on the lines over the interior courtyard, a pair of trainers where you'd be likely to trip over them. On the walls are black and white photographs of figures moving through huge landscapes with distant grey hills in the background. The pictures are a tribute to Marce's attachment to some romantic notion of Argentina.

Wide pampas, solitary horseman in poncho and leather brimmed hat. On the dining-room table, several books: a couple of broken-spined novels, and some fat volumes with titles like *Stalingrad* or *A History of Europe since 1945*.

'That's yours.' He points to the little bedroom. 'Laura made me change the sheets.'

'Cheers,' I say. 'I see you've got a couple of books on the go, then.'

'I like to flit from one to the other. Your typical autodidact – superficially knowledgeable over a wide range of topics.'

'Still, more than I can claim.'

Soon I feel comfortable being here. It's like returning to those years we spent on the calle Fúcar, back in the noughties. We've been through a lot together since. In that gruelling trek through the Baltics, he provided most of the rare moments of relief, fun even. We had our conflicts – some of them existential, almost terminal – but on the whole, I can safely say I wouldn't have made it back without him.

I lie on the narrow bed in Marce's flat, hands behind my head. I'm still having flashbacks to the fear and despair when I thought all was lost. Post-traumatic stress the psychologists would call it, not that I go near them after my counselling fiasco. But there were moments of joy too. Like the time I bumped into Marce on the ferry across the lagoon at

Klaipeda. Standing there, with bags under his eyes, looking like a tramp – it was so, so wonderful to see him. Once we'd docked, I remember, we sat in a little park and ate some of the food Kamilė had given me. 'Fucking delectable, this salami,' Marce said, while I wrapped it in its greaseproof paper, because he was capable of polishing it off in one go.

'How did you get away?' I asked.

He told me, and my brief elation turned back to despair. 'Everyone out safely, but as soon as we hit the road they spotted us. Sheer bad luck. Piled us into the back of the Warriors. Pro-Russian militias to judge by the Cyrillic lettering. One of ours made a run for it, they shot him through the neck. Georgescu, the cook.'

'Christ almighty. Georgescu made a run for it? Brave man.'

'Yeah. Lousy cook, brave man. So the rest of us weren't going to argue. They drove the trucks onto the sand, pulled everyone out. I got dumped down on the edge, nearest the tree-line. There was some argument between the militiamen, probably over who got what. I just got up and ran for the trees, and kept running. Heard a lot of shooting. Poor sods. So what now, *mi capitán*, what's the plan? What would a good *cristiano* do in our situation? Or a bad Jew?'

Marce's certainly a bad Jew. But he's quite clear about being a Jew and he's proud of it. Profane and non-practising, but still, defiantly, a Jew. I'd say to him, 'You don't give a damn about religion, do you? Don't go to synagogue, you eat pork and *gambas*, yet if anyone dares call you a dirty yid, like that fellow did at naval college, I remember, you smack them in the face with a pickaxe handle.'

'You can talk!' he'd say. He'd be referring to the time I was reprimanded for punching the hell out of someone who'd taken to calling me 'cripple dick' when he discovered I was circumcised. Was probably Marce's example that made me do it. 'What I don't understand,' I said at the time, 'is why I'm singled out for attention. You're also circumcised yet they don't start on you.' He said, 'Because they're struck by the splendour of my *partes nobles*.' And to my guffaw he added, 'And because I make an effort to be basically affable towards my fellow trainees and – unlike you – try to hide my belief I'm superior to everyone else.'

Sure, there were one or two unpleasant incidents in naval college, but apart from that I enjoyed the experience. Even the Galician drizzle couldn't get me down, because I was so delighted to be out of Madrid and away from my gloomy family. I began to carve out my own path. My classmates still saw me as an outsider but they came to respect me, especially after the cripple-dick incident. And I did well in the leadership exercises. When called upon, I could take teams on week-long training hikes across the *meseta* in forty degrees, or on difficult missions skiing through whiteouts on the Picos de Europa. I worked out how to keep my men together, urge them on when they were running out of steam. Could make the tough calls. Had a knack for achieving goals, reaching the destination. I could be abrupt in command, but pretty effective.

Marce was my only friend at college. A strange alliance, attraction of opposites. He was so laid-back, frivolous, low on guilt and principles. Always with a wry, disillusioned take on naval life and the wider world. Whereas I was driven, mission-focused, grim-faced; at least in public. We'd joke about who'd be first to command a battlecruiser. He was a skinny Sancho Panza to my Quijote, or so he'd tell me (*Don Quijote* being one of the many indispensable books I haven't read). He could make me laugh – still can – and tell me plainly that I'm behaving like an idiot. He's a bit of a bundle of contradictions. I suppose we all are.

19.

The Jewish thing. Margalit and I have had endless discussions about it. I remember the angst we went through when Rubén was born. She'd have liked a traditional circumcision in synagogue with all the attendant ritual.

'It represents a covenant with God. The official, the *mohel*, takes the infant, lays him on a surface, makes the cut, extracts a spot of blood. Simple, powerful. It's the symbolism, it marks you out. Says you belong, you're part of this community.'

It sounded barbaric to me. So I had a word with Simón Guinsburg. He and his wife Alejandra are old friends of Margalit's. Like Marce, Simón is the son of Jewish immigrants who – along with many others – fled to Spain from Argentina during the period of the military Junta in the 1970s. He's a genito-urinary surgeon who sometimes acts as *mohel* for Spain's Ashkenazi community. His wife Alejandra is also a doctor.

'You *can* be a Jew and not be circumcised,' said Simón. 'In earlier times, they didn't remove all the foreskin, it was something much more discreet.'

He explained that in the second century BCE, the rabbis decreed the extreme version. 'Why would they want to? To remove the temptation for Jews to restore their foreskin. Which they wanted to do so they could go and exercise nude at the *gymnasium* and show off their beautiful foreskins. Like the Greeks.'

'Yes, absolutely, that would be top of my agenda, too,' I said.

Simón smiled indulgently. 'So,' he continued, 'I'm saying Rubencito could have a minor circumcision, and that would do fine.'

'But why do it at all?'

'First, you need to be circumcised to do your bar mitzvah, marry within the community, and so on. Second, because that's what Margalit wants.'

'At least they don't cut the women in Judaism.'

Simón winced. 'I've had to repair the damage of female genital mutilation. It's about controlling women's sexuality.'

I said, with a straight face, 'So how does a Jew control his woman's sexuality?'

Simón gave me a look that said *how come I'm friends with this guy?* Then he saw me grin, and laughed and said, 'By being a fantastic lover, David!', and slapped me on the shoulder.

Margalit and I argued for days before agreeing to settle for Simón's proposal: a minimalist 'pre-Babylonian' circumcision. We both felt we were giving away more than we'd have wished. 'That, my friends,' said Simón, 'is the essence of compromise.'

He performed the procedure in hospital and presented us with a certificate bearing the details of the parents, and the name in Hebrew and Spanish of the infant: 'Rubén Eliécer *ben* David'.

I worried for years my son was now mutilated, as I'd been. Sometime later, Margalit told me that she still found the unorthodox procedure difficult to accept.

'I wish I'd held out for a proper circumcision, with a proper ceremony, in synagogue. And I can't get out of my head this image of our boy, little Rubén, not so little, undressing in front of his first Jewish partner, and the girl throws up her hands in horror or shrieks or something. Because his bits aren't like those of other men.'

I laughed. 'Sounds quite experienced, this hypothetical girlfriend of our Rubén.'

'Don't be facetious, David, I'm serious. Girls talk about these things among themselves, and, you know...'

'Talk about their man's dick?'

'You'd be surprised.'

'So do you talk about me and my penis with your girlfriends, darling?' I asked, and the conversation took an unintended detour into male insecurities.

I can cope with the Jewish festivals, or at least the less sombre ones. I'm not big on blowing ram's horns and fasting and so on. I had enough of the rituals of penitence growing up in a Catholic household; I wasn't going to take on someone else's self-scourging. But I do like the more upbeat, family-oriented festivals: Pesach, Hanukkah, Purim especially. I look forward to them with a curious mixture of belonging and distance. Sometimes, I feel like an anthropologist observing peculiar rites in the heart of the exotic clan that is my own family. At other times, I don't feel like an outsider at all, I feel part of proceedings.

Take Hanukkah, the festival with the candelabra and the lights, representing the sacred oil in the Temple in Jerusalem. The oil didn't run out, supposedly – a miracle. The tradition is to eat lots of oily foods and cheese.

'They certainly stuff themselves on cheesy pancakes,' I'd say, disapprovingly, in the early days, when I was on home leave from wherever. 'Not to mention all the other sugary, deep-fried *bimuelos* and the rest.' 'For eight days, David,' Margalit would say. 'It's not going to do them too much harm.'

Anyway, the oil isn't what engages me as far as Hanukkah goes. It's the story of the Jews' heroic resistance to the Macedonian overlords of Israel (or were they Syrians, I was never quite clear on that) who forbade Jews from practising their religion. As Sara would explain to me with relish, year after year, as we sat round the dinner table on the first night of Hanukkah, the Macedonians desecrated the Temple 'by sacrificing pigs on the holy altar!'

'Pigs? No!' I'd say, sensing Margalit's eyes on me, her ironic smile.

'And they tortured people to death for refusing to eat pig, didn't they, *mami*? Or for having their sons circumcised. And they murdered Jewish boy children. Rubencito, they'd have killed him definitely.'

She knew that Rubencito would aim a kick under the table, which she would easily dodge.

'But the Jews fought back, didn't they?' Margalit would say, to move things on before they got out of hand. 'With their big hero, Judah Maccabee.'

At which point, Rubencito would cry out, 'Yes! Yes!' and when he was quite young he'd pick up a fork and stab the air and make angry noises and shout, 'Kill all our enemies!' until his mother gently shushed him.

'Very good, Rubencito,' she said. 'Judah Maccabee and his men drove out the Macedonians, and the Jews could worship again in the Temple in Jerusalem.'

Now, Sarita was saying as she did every year, 'And, remind us why we eat oily foods, *mami*, and the cheese, and all that.'

Margalit countered, 'Why don't you tell us, *cariño*.'

'All right,' said Sarita, knowing her lines in this performance. She'd bend low over the table as she'd seen her mother do in past years, and she'd go, 'This is about the oil in the Temple, and also about remembering the heroine, Judith, who pretended to be the girlfriend of an enemy general.'

'Called Holofernes.'

'Yes, whatever. And she gave him lots of incredibly salty cheese to make him really thirsty so he had to drink lots of wine and he fell fast asleep. And when he was sleeping,' – she paused dramatically before crying in a rush – 'she took an axe and chopped his head off!' She banged her hand down on the table.

Margalit would make big round surprised eyes and say, 'Is that really what happened?'

'I'd love to cut some enemy general's head off when I grow up,' Sara said.

'And me, and me,' Rubén added, launching puny karate chops in all directions.

Margalit would beam at me proudly, and I'd smile back, with a warm, cossetted feeling. Over time, we'd reached a messy, shifting compromise on my Jewishness. Before I met her, it was a fact, uncomfortable and odd, that I could stash away and forget about. Once we were together, I couldn't just ignore it. Especially after Margalit met Elena and the two women would gabble away like close relatives reunited after a long separation. They formed an alliance to get me to acknowledge my Jewish heritage.

So, our compromise: Rubén had been duly circumcised, if not entirely to Margalit's liking, nor mine. We held family celebrations for the major festivals. I made occasional guest appearances in synagogue. Seafood wasn't allowed in the house, pig meat an unbreakable taboo. For me, this last was a sacrifice too far – I'd have had no problem with the Macedonians' edict about having to eat pigs. So while I respect the ban at home, I still periodically nip out to bars and gorge on *jamón de jabugo* and *chorizo* and *gambas al ajillo*. It's part of my birthright, if you like. By tacit agreement, Margalit and I have stopped discussing it. *Don't ask, don't tell.* It seems to work.

Talking of ham, it reminds me of a little episode of light relief with Marce in Lithuania. About a week into our trek, we spent the night as usual in some mucky barn, and woke to find a trembling youth pointing an ancient shotgun at us. Then his mother and other kids and an old man turned up. Marce talked the lad into putting the shotgun down. They were starving, the lot of them. I gave them the remains of the *skilandis* Kamilė had given me for the journey. We're back on the road, it's cold and damp, and Marce says, 'Those poor bastards were going to starve anyway, so why give them the fucking salami!

We've just prolonged their agony.' Marce at his most magnanimous and humanitarian. I say, 'It was pork, Feigenbaum, it was pork,' and we both laugh. 'Not eating all the pork, that's my Jewishness in action.' The laughter kept us going, even if he was right, we could really have done with the sustenance. I guess it was an act on my part of *gemilut hasidim* – good works – that Margalit's always going on about as being one of the core principles of Judaism.

20.

This morning I've come to see Elena again. I've brought some pastries from Punto Dulce. She smiles, puts them on the kitchen counter, absently, and asks about Margalit and me.

'Oh, you know, we're working things through.'

'Good. I hope so.'

There are so many things I need to talk to my mother about and we're running out of time. I'm very conscious Margalit knows where she comes from. I feel I need to offer her something similar from my side, and Elena is a perfect informant. We've talked before, of course, about her history – which is also mine – but not very systematically. I'd like to fill in some of the gaps.

So we've sat down in armchairs in the living room of her flat, facing each other, and I've got her chatting about her childhood. I can see through to the dining room, the silver sabbath candlesticks on the table.

She's uncomfortable and in pain, but happy to talk. In her memory, her youth was idyllic, she was her father's favourite.

'We were so close even my mother felt cut out sometimes. So I was completely devastated when he disowned me. After the… affair, you know.'

She winces in pain.

'Have you got your medication?'

'Oh yes. But sometimes I like to have clarity. It's a trade-off – less pain, more brain fog.'

I laugh, and so does she, with a grimace. On the wall is a framed reproduction, a painting of a rabbi with a prayer shawl over his head, all harsh blacks and whites. Above the fireplace, another of a young woman, with a long neck and long dark hair, dressed in blue. For a brief moment it crosses my mind that it's Elena in her youth, but then I see the girl's brooch, in the shape of a cross, so it can't be her.

'I've so many memories of a happy Jewish childhood,' she continues. 'Like lighting candles for Shabbat. Supposed to be the woman of the household, but my father usually talked my mother into letting me light them. Oh, the eggy taste of the *challah* bread with poppy seeds my mum used to make. Helping her do the *folares* for Purim.'

'*Folares*?'

Elena looks at me like this is something I should know by now. 'Pastries. You wrap hard-boiled eggs in strips of dough and bake them. It's a very Sephardi thing.'

'Oh yes, Margalit makes them with Sarita. I didn't know they were called that.'

'I always used to get more flour on the floor than in the bowl.'

'You got dressed up and that sort of thing?'

'Yes, long skirts, gold-coloured cloths wrapped round my head, like I was Queen Esther and was going to save the Jews from the wicked Haman. I'm sure Sarita dresses up in her mother's clothes.'

'I guess so, though she's a bit too old and stroppy for that these days.'

'It's a phase, *cariño*. She'll grow out of it.'

I grunt.

'Sara's mirroring you and your reaction to her. Relax a bit and the stakes will be less.'

'You're right, I should let it wash over me. But she sure knows how to touch a nerve.'

'It's what teenagers are genetically programmed to do.'

'That's what Margalit says.'

Elena gazes without seeing. 'I remember a lot of stuff. Mostly of me with my father. Walking to the new Jewish community centre for the morning service on Shabbat, skipping along with my arm through his. They made me sit with the ladies, but I wanted to sit with him. All my friends thought synagogue was boring but I didn't. When the scrolls of the Torah came out of the Ark, you know, and they unrolled them on the *bimah*, it was exciting. I'd wonder how long it took the scribe to do all that beautiful Hebrew writing on the goatskin, and so neatly. Years. What happens if you're a scribe and you make a mistake? Do you have to go back and start again from scratch?'

'Sounds like a really stressful occupation. Very niche. And very heavy on goats.'

'Yes, must be.' She chuckles: more a smily gasp, with that pained grimace at the end of it. 'Sometimes the cantor came and led the congregation in singing *Shemá Yisrael*. I'd get goosebumps, it was like the whole air was electric...'

Elena takes a dose of morphine from a dark bottle, and relaxes again.

'You okay?'

'I'm sorry, *cariño*, after a while I need to take the edge off. Just help me into bed.'

When she's settled, sitting up against the pillows, I ask, 'What did your father do for a living?' She's probably told me before, but it's not information I've retained. Now it seems more pressing to know these things. 'Not a rabbi, was he?' I add, gesturing to the painting.

She laughs. 'Goodness me, no. My father – your grandfather – worked in local government, here in Madrid.'

'Yes, of course. Like you did.'

My grandfather, I thought, the marvellous idea that I had a lineage going back beyond Elena.

'In the planning office, to do with budgets or accounts. Or something, I don't know. His father had been a sales rep for a leather goods firm, travelling round Greece and Yugoslavia with samples in a suitcase. But my dad and I didn't talk about his own childhood that much. I wish we had. And in later years when we became reconciled, we were preoccupied with other things, like his and my mother's failing health.'

'You were reconciled with him?'

'Yes, we both admitted we'd made mistakes. If we hadn't been so stubborn and resentful, the pair of us, we'd probably have been reconciled much earlier.'

'What sort of man was he, my grandfather?'

'Very proud of his eyebrows.' We grin at the randomness of the memory. 'Very thick and black, they were, a nice arch to them. Rather like yours, in fact. He'd snip off any stray hairs with a pair of scissors when he thought no one was looking.'

'I do that,' I say. 'Margalit thinks it's hilarious.'

She pulls up the duvet to cover her chest. 'You know, something I never realised as a kid: he had a foreign accent until the day he died.'

'My grandfather? He wasn't Spanish?'

'Not for about twelve generations. He came to Spain during the war, from Bulgaria, aged thirteen.

One of the lucky ones. His Sephardi name saved him and his parents, because it allowed the Spanish ambassador in Sofia to protect them. A staunch Francoist, imagine! He stood up to the Nazis. The last person you'd expect.'

'Why did he do it?'

'The ambassador? He said out of "Christian charity". Where would we Jews be without it!'

I think for a moment she's being facetious, but she isn't.

'I'm getting tired, *cariño*. I think I'll sleep.'

I bend down so she can kiss my cheek.

'*Ay, ay, ay*, that's what the Sephardis are: Spaniards without a homeland.'

'You still feel that?'

'In a way, yes. You never know what's coming next.'

'What? Pogroms, expulsions? That kind of thing.'

'All right, you may mock,' she says. 'It's unlikely, I know. But these things are unthinkable... until they happen. Everything's provisional, even things that seem stable. Don't forget that.'

I rub her shoulder fondly. 'I'll try not to, *mamá*.'

'Off you go, you impudent rascal!'

21.

I don't think I'd want paintings of rabbis on the wall at home. But Margalit has made sure there's still a Jewish vibe to our flat. Sitting on the living-room sofa at Marce's now, I can visualise the antique silver menorah candlestick, for example, brought down from its high shelf and given a good polish a day or two before Hanukkah starts. Or a porcelain spinning top with Hebrew lettering, from some distant relative, relegated to the second loo. Decorated ceramic plates from Israel, mounted on stands on the dining-room bookcase. Volumes on Jewish history, of course, in the study, some of them with forests of yellow Post-it notes sticking out. A large old black and white photograph of Jerusalem in the hallway. In our bedroom, a framed reproduction that I used to think was rather old-fashioned, but which I've grown to love: a man and a woman in the wedding finery of their time, in creams and orangey-reds, a Jewish bridal couple according to Margalit.

They seem so close in their bond – she's touching his hand delicately with hers, and she looks a bit pensive; but perhaps it's their wedding night. I guess Margalit feels that gentle exposure to these things, reminders of Jewishness, will help me feel it more. I do miss having the objects around me. The decorations in Marce's flat, Argentinian landscapes and all, don't have that same sense of… familiarity.

In our early days, she tried to educate me. Handed me books on Judaism, which I started and gave up. Or sat me down and talked about the five books of Moses, the prophets, the festivals, principles of the Jewish faith. Some of it stuck. She showed me videos on the history of the Sephardis, on the Holocaust, even Israeli television dramas. All very interesting. None of it touched me as much as I hoped.

'They were victims,' I'd say. 'I'm not a victim. Always being picked on, aren't they, the Jews. Like the weak, nerdy boy in the playground.'

'Not always, darling. Sometimes they stand and fight. Look at the Warsaw ghetto. Judah Maccabee. Hardly victims.'

She came to the conclusion it was practice I needed, not theory, and began to take me to synagogue for the Shabbat service. She tried to ignore the stares of those who still resented her break-up with Arturo.

'In their eyes, you're not even a proper Jew.'

'Screw them! I'm circumcised, aren't I? What's their problem?'

'We're not married in synagogue, remember.'

'Only because your arsehole of a husband refused to grant you some piece of paper stamped by the rabbi.'

'And also because you weren't bar-mitzvahed. In any case, you're hardly a Jew from the inside out, as it were.'

She's right about that. If I hadn't been with her, I'd probably have let the Jewish part of my identity fade away altogether.

The synagogue's above the Jewish community centre. Red brick exterior, great concrete bollards outside the main entrance – presumably to deter terrorists. I think I expected something more spiritual. Modern stained-glass windows along one wall, dark-wood panelling, an elaborate central light, like a giant spinning top. Margalit tells me it represents the 'eternal light', the everlasting oil lamp in the Temple in Jerusalem.

I was surprised how many young people attended. And when the cantor led the Sabbath prayers, I felt a frisson of recognition, like hearing the priest in Mass. I thought back almost nostalgically to the church of San Fermín de Navarros near the family home, forgetting for a moment the tedium of those endless services.

Once, walking back from the Sabbath morning service along Eloy Gonzalo, we passed a member of the congregation Margalit vaguely recognised. An older man, wearing a fedora at a jaunty angle. She nodded a greeting. He blanked her and spat into the gutter. She said, outraged, 'Did you see that, David?'

'I saw it. Do you want me to—'

'Do what – your scary man act?'

'No, of course not.'

She took my hand. 'At least make an effort to understand how it is for me.'

'I know. You're sacrificing things on my behalf. I see that, absolutely. That was one unpleasant individual, they're not all like that.'

'No, but the community makes you pay.'

'So why do we still go along to Shabbat services?'

'David, it's what I know, it's what I was brought up with.' She pouted comically. 'I sometimes feel I'm a free-floating Jew, for Christ's sake!'

'Like in those Chagall paintings you introduced me to, with bridal couples wafting through the air?' This image was in my mind of Chagall's sinister giant chickens: why did they crop up in pictures of airborne brides?

'Yes, free-floating. Bit of a contradiction, if you think about it. Because even in the worst days of the Inquisition, the *marranos* weren't free-floating, they were anchored, always in contact with other clandestine Jews. Some of them got burned alive for their pains.'

'I don't consider myself a coward, *mi amor*, but being burned alive would not be one of my priorities.'

'At least they had a sense of belonging.'

I remember one evening we were round at Simón and Alejandra's, it would be mid-2010s, and I asked them what the essence of Jewishness was. Some core I could grasp and, I don't know, *perform*.

Alejandra said, 'Part of it's about just getting on with it. Getting by. Surviving. And traditions, family.' She gestured to the laden table. 'All this stuff.'

'It's not necessarily going to synagogue every week,' said Simón, 'knowing how to wrap the prayer shawl round you and recite *Shemá Yisrael* by heart while rocking backwards and forwards. It's not about that.'

'For me,' said Margalit, 'the essence is trying to do good acts, *gemilut hasidim*. Trying to live by the code of the Torah, or whatever code you live by.'

'In your case, David,' said Simón, 'maybe it's about trying to live by your version of military ethics.'

'If that isn't a contradiction in terms,' said Alejandra.

I was about to object to her remark, when Simón asked, 'How does it feel, being a Jew in the military?'

'Feel? In what way?'

Simón laughed. 'Ah, a genuine Jew, answering a question with a question. I mean, is there a tension there?'

'It's not been an issue,' I said, defensively, even as I remembered the bullying I'd endured at the naval academy. 'When I'm on-board ship, I have my role and get on with it, like everyone else. Catholic, Muslim, Jew. For my crew, I'm the commanding officer, not "the Jew". As for being a *genuine* Jew, I don't know what that even means. I'm a bad Jew, that's for sure.'

'Really?' said Alejandra.

'Yes. I mean, you can't suddenly stop being Catholic if that's how you were brought up. It colours the way you see the world. Then you suddenly find out you're a Jew, in my case in my late twenties. A bit late in the day to ditch your whole cultural baggage that you've had since childhood, and build up something new, new traditions and all that.'

I sat back, surprised at myself. Perhaps it was the warmth of our hosts, the glasses of wine, that had created this confessional atmosphere.

'Never too late,' said Simón.

'I'm afraid,' I said, 'I'm not even sure I believe in God.'

Margalit said, 'Look, darling, it's not necessary to believe in God to be a Jew. There are Jews who do and Jews who don't, but they're still Jews.'

'I thought you told me that the basic principles of Judaism were, number one, believe in God.'

'Ach, principles!' she said airily. 'Being Jewish is about so much more than principles.'

'Going back to Simón's earlier point,' said Alejandra, 'a Jewish soldier, or even a soldier as in your case who's a little bit Jewish, is an unusual combination, in Spain at least. And raises all the usual questions. If you're a Jew, who are you fighting for? Like the Dreyfus affair: can a Jew be a Jew and also a loyal Frenchman? Or Spaniard, or European, for that matter?'

I said, 'The Dreyfus case was over a century ago.'

'Remember, he wasn't even a practising Jew. Being assimilated didn't save him. The French establishment didn't make the fine distinction. Neither, of course, did the Nazis.'

'Exactly,' said Margalit. 'Members of my family in Salonica wouldn't have recognised a Torah scroll if it fell on them, but off they went to Auschwitz just the same...'

'We're not expecting another holocaust any time soon, are we?'

'Look around you,' said Alejandra. 'You're the military man. You can see that Europe's fraying at the edges. Starts small, but it adds up, doesn't it. Small wars in faraway Chechnya, faraway Georgia, and now shaping up nicely in the Baltics. Cyber-attacks, fake news. Messing with elections, politicians ranting and raving and spouting hate. On top of that, economic uncertainty. Who knows where it's all leading.' She sounded like Marce at his most grandiose.

'This paranoia I just don't get,' I said. 'The idea you need to keep a suitcase packed because the good times won't last, and sooner or later "they" will be coming for you.'

'Is it paranoia, though? You can see the inflammatory language, the rallies, the poisonous atmosphere. Not a huge leap from being anti-foreigner to being anti-Jew.'

I thought about it for a moment. 'I suppose, to the anti-Semite, a bad Jew is a tautology. All Jews are bad Jews.'

'Yes indeed,' said Alejandra.

'Which means that as Jews go, I'm no worse than other Jews!' I laughed. The others joined in.

'Correct!'

Margalit once told me, 'When you laugh, it's like a bishop dancing the tango!' She added, 'You could try doing it more often.' As far as I'm concerned, it comes when it comes, it's not something you can turn on and off. When we're alone, she says, I'm warm and engaging and I smile. She loves seeing my mumbling embarrassment, and the grin I can't quite suppress.

Margalit looked at her phone. 'Darling, it's late, we should let these good people get to bed.'

'It's fine,' said Simón.

'So what's the answer?' I asked. 'About what it means to be a Jew.'

Simón chuckled. 'The essence is, as Rabbi Akiva said, when some schmuck asks you to summarise the key tenets of the Torah while standing on one leg,

"Do not do unto others that which you would not have done unto yourself." The golden rule.'

I nodded. 'Touché. As Catholics would say, do as you would be done by. But I never said you had to stand on one leg.'

'Fair enough.'

'All right, that's enough for one evening,' said Margalit.

'You're right,' said Simón. 'But just to sum up, we have a Jew who probably doesn't believe in God, probably isn't going to go to synagogue much, am I right? Maybe the odd Shabbat or high holy day service. Who's a military officer, possibly with a code of military ethics... Or not. So where does that leave us?'

Were they expecting me to talk about *gemilut hasidim* on the battlefield, no man left behind, all that? They were looking at me with raised eyebrows. Waiting, I felt, for me to resolve the tricky question.

'Where does that leave us?' I repeated. 'God knows. God only knows.'

'Exactly!' said Alejandra.

'Come on,' Margalit said. 'Home.'

22.

Van Raalte is on FaceTime again, quizzing me about the overland trek through the Baltic states.

'So it was just you and Lieutenant Feigenbaum? No other crew members?'

'And our interpreter.'

'Your interpreter? From the patrol boat?'

'No, no. Mr Irbe. Kaspars Irbe. Freelance. We came upon him by chance. About two weeks into the hike. He needed protection. We needed someone who knew the language and the terrain.'

I don't fill in the details – it would just make van Raalte's eyebrows shoot up and his head slide despairingly further down his screen; Irbe was, shall we say, something of a wildcard.

We were north-east of Klaipėda, on a country road, when we found this wrecked mansion, probably once belonging to some Russian oligarch. The place was a mess – broken floors, crumbling staircases, goats in the hallway, animal and human shit everywhere, bloodstained walls. It had been looted but we found a sack of grain and some tins in the kitchen, along with a fearsomely sharp cook's knife. In the basement was a collection of big-finned old American cars from the sixties, rusting away.

Marce swept his arm round the exhibits and spouted off about 'The Great American dream of iconic consumerism, no? Especially if you grew up with Trabants and Tatras in pre-1989 eastern Europe.' We heard a metallic scrape, then a groan. A figure rose between two rusting Corvairs, hands held high. A scarecrow of a man, pot-bellied, naked except for an improvised loincloth. Hair and beard matted into dreadlocks, eyes bright blue.

Marce shouted to him to kneel on the floor, in English and German. The guy complied. 'Americans?'

'No, Europeans,' said Marce. 'We're Spanish. From EuDeFor.'

'Ah, *Die Europäische Friedenskraft. Sehr gut. Ausgezeichnet!*'

I rasped, in my imperfect English, 'What is your name?'

The guy attempted to kneel straighter, making his pot belly bulge. 'My name is Kaspars Irbe. And yours, if I may ask?' He reached out as if to shake my hand.

'Don't fucking move,' said Marce.

'What are you doing here?' I asked.

He grinned. His lower teeth, where he still had them, were crooked and yellow. 'I am Latvian, from the town of Grobiņa. In addition to Latvian language, I am fluent in Lithuanian, Russian, English and of course German, and therefore useful. So perhaps it is better if you do not shoot me, yes?'

'Fair enough,' said Marce. 'You can stand up now.'

Irbe told us he'd been abducted by Gorynych's men, as if we were supposed to know who Gorynych was. Some kind of militia leader, apparently. Wanted an independent republic of ethnic Russians across a strip of Lithuania and Latvia. 'In another life, Gorynych was funeral director.'

The militiamen threatened violence against his wife and family, he said, if he didn't go with them as interpreter. 'And now I have nowhere to go, because...'

He clamped his arms around his chest and shivered. Then he pointed to the nest of filthy blankets and said, 'May I?', and bent down and retrieved a scuffed photograph. It was of a dark-haired woman and two young children lying dead on the roadside with bullet wounds. His family? He nodded. 'Gorynych did this.'

Marce and I exchanged glances. A weird individual, but no threat.

'Europe is idea in the minds of fools,' he said. When we didn't respond, he continued. 'Five languages I speak, and that does not make me European.'

It made me think of our lost crew. The cook, Georgescu, Romanian from Constanța. The second lieutenant, de Vries, from Apeldoorn. Malling from Århus. Cordeiro from Coimbra. Helme from Tallin. Khaled from Marseilles, Quintana from Vigo. And so on, from thirteen different countries of the continent, men and women working together. That was Europe. Not some abstraction.

We discussed what to do with him. It was easy for me to think of *gemilut hasidim* and suggest we take the poor guy with us. He'd seen his whole family butchered, or so he said. But I was also thinking he might be of use, with his languages and knowledge of the region. Marce was against taking him. 'Look at the state of him, he'll only hold us back. And he could be spinning us a line.'

The next morning we were jolted awake by a pistol shot and ran to the window. Irbe was standing on what was once the lawn, beside the body of a goat. Looked up, saw us, and gave us a thumbs up. Marce shouted out of the window. 'You bloody moron! All militias within ten kilometres will come running.'

I said to Marce, 'He's a stray bullet. He'll cause us grief.'

'With respect, you've changed your tune, Captain. Going on about the right thing to do, now you want to leave him to rot? Look, you said it, he could be our interpreter. Without him we might as well be on Mars. We just have to keep an eye on him. Kick him if he steps out of line.'

When we came out with our sparse belongings, Irbe was kneeling on the ground next to the goat, kitchen knife in hand. He held up a haunch, peeled the hide off it like a glove. '*Et voilà!*' he said. 'I gift it you. The rest I put in basement to keep me alive until the militias return…'

'Lord Almighty, preserve us,' murmured Marce.

'Okay, so he knows how to skin and gut a goat.'

We looked at each other, and at the steaming pile of goat's intestines.

'A useful skill.'

So that was how we both agreed Irbe could come with us, out of base pragmatism; and we both agreed we'd dump him as soon as he became a burden. So much for *gemilut hasidim.*

Van Raalte is saying, 'And you're sure of the bona fides of this…' – consults his notes – '…*Irb*?'

'Irbe,' I say. 'Yes, absolutely. Both Lieutenant Feigenbaum and I are EuDeFor-trained interrogators. He was clearly no foreign agent, and was a highly qualified linguist.' As Marce had joked at the time, 'He speak five languages, and English the wellest.'

'Very good,' says van Raalte. 'So now you are three.'

'Yes, and we make the rest of the journey together.'

'Tell me, Captain,' he asks, his body shifting upwards on the screen of my mobile. 'What's that peculiar object on the table behind you?'

'Oh, that's just Lieutenant Feigenbaum's *mate* gourd, from Argentina. He drinks his *mate* tea out of it.'

'I see,' says van Raalte.

'Through a silver straw.'

'Very good.'

23.

I go for a long walk up to La Latina and back down through Lavapiés. Many non-Spanish faces, guys standing around in one of the little squares, in T-shirts even though it's cold. The side streets a hotbed of crime and drug-dealing, allegedly. On the home leg, I cross the main road and come out opposite the railway museum. There's a poster at the entrance advertising an exhibition of tilting trains, the famous Talgo. It brings back a childhood memory of my father. He was a Talgo enthusiast and brought me here not long after the museum opened. I must have been ten or eleven. He said we'd go on a Talgo trip with my mother. It never came to anything. As he got older, he hated leaving Madrid, especially on public transport.

I think I was his cover for that museum outing. 'It'll be educational for the lad,' he said to Rocío. I'd have preferred the Naval Museum, even though I'd been three or four times already. I loved its models of old warships in glass cases, and its paintings of great naval battles on stormy seas against a backdrop of enormous skies.

Back at Marce's flat now. My morning walk has only confirmed what I already knew: I shouldn't be here. I should be at home in Chamberí, sorting things out with Margalit. I hear from her, mainly businesslike phone calls or WhatsApp messages about the household and the kids. Sara is at Arturo's. The plumber's coming on Wednesday. Rubén is not doing as well as he should at school (an implied note of criticism, that I'm an absent father). And a recent text: 'Just to remind everyone that my book launch is on the 10th! Hugs, M.' It's clearly been sent to her whole contact list, but at least she didn't exclude me. I know we should talk, I should earn my right to return home, but my head's still in the Baltics.

The frequent flashbacks leave me harrowed and out of sorts. I talked to Margalit when I first returned, and she'd make sympathetic noises. But she hasn't lived through what I lived through. She can't know what you feel when you see the dead bodies of your crew members, your charges. She can't understand your overwhelming feelings of having let your people down, even though you haven't. Or your abject terror when you're at the mercy of militia thugs, who've already beaten you, cracked a few ribs and a cheekbone, and who could beat you to a pulp again at any moment. Or how you're past caring when you have to shit in your clothes, where you lie, because the militiaman's standing over you, rifle butt readied, and refusing to let you go to the bushes (not that you could take your trousers down anyway, with zip ties on your wrists). How you're so weary you're not even sure that you're frightened about another beating. How almost as bad as the physical stuff and the dirt is your humiliation when they go through your phone, mocking the photos of your wife, making obscene gestures, and you're powerless to do anything about it.

She tried to brush it off. 'Darling, they're just photos, don't be so angry.' That's the wrong thing to say. The rage of it is still with me, and I don't know what do with it. I wake up grinding my teeth and with a desire to scrunch my tormentors' faces into a concrete floor, and for the whole morning my jaw aches.

Even if she has a sense that it was all traumatic, she can't grasp the *texture* of the everyday things. Only Marce understands. Those long weeks of the two of us alone against the world: that binds you together, changes you, makes it hard to adapt back to 'ordinary' life. All the mundane ways of being cold, scared, hungry and exhausted become your new normal. I don't know how to get that across to Margalit.

When I think back on our ordeal in calmer moments, it's often the little things that come to mind. Like the salami episode. Or when we found a freezing church in a deserted village. Pews for beds

– luxury. Earlier, we'd dug up some potatoes. Marce produced a fire-lighting kit with some kindling and lighters from his coat pocket, like a magician. 'Was saving it up for a special occasion.' Got a fire going, packed the potatoes in the base, boiled some ditch water in an old can. After an hour, we picked the baked potatoes from the embers and ate them, burned skins and still-hard cores and all.

'I needed that,' Marce said, 'though as birthday meals go...'

'It's your birthday?'

'If it's the 28th, *sí, señor*. Forty-two years old. *Salud, dinero y amor*. Our health's crap, money's useless and, hey, who needs love!'

We clinked our makeshift metal cups of hot water. 'Happy birthday, man, happy birthday! If I'd have known, I'd have sent out to Lhardy's for pastries.' I wondered then if I'd be home with my family in time for my next birthday, or ever.

When the world's falling apart around you, these small moments matter. But the tight little cell we formed during our trek is now a hindrance, a blockage between me and Margalit. The only person I might have asked for advice is Elena, but she's too unwell. I regret that now she's dying, and I've not made the most of her being around. With her links to the past, she might have stopped me feeling so, I don't know... untethered.

24.

Today, I heard from EuDeFor. Marce has an identical letter with the same postmark. We're summoned to report to naval headquarters, northern division, to be questioned about the sinking of the Pandora with the loss of most of its crew. The HQ's in Kiel, on Germany's Baltic coast.

Van Raalte says again that we need to get our story straight. Thank you, *Licenciado*, we'd already worked that one out. We did the right things. But luck has so much to do with it. Our people were so unlucky. Marce was lucky to escape. I was lucky I found him.

'You decided to march overland?' van Raalte says.

'Yes. Trek round in a wide semicircle, couple of hundred kilometres, to avoid the worst of the fighting and the militias.'

'But you were captured by a militia group?'

'Yes, some weeks in. But we escaped.'

'What can you tell me about the militias?'

'They were pro-Russian, anti-Russian, I don't know.'

'The inquiry will want to know.'

'We were worried about staying alive. Not gathering intel.'

Van Raalte looks at me over his spectacles. 'And you escaped how? You will be asked that.'

I know, I know. Rubén has been asking exactly that for weeks.

When it comes to the looming shipwreck that is my personal life, Margalit is likely to be a sterner judge than any retired rear admiral in Kiel chairing some plodding commission of inquiry. There's the question, as always, of my Jewishness.

'And you, darling,' she'd say, 'what kind of Jew are you? If any?'

'What do you want me to *do*?'

'Something more than treat it as topic for intellectual debate round the Guinsburgs' dinner table.'

Sometimes those debates could become edgy, because they confirmed for Margalit that I was a half-hearted sort of Jew. She had a cousin, Gideon, who was an officer in the Israeli Defence Forces.

'The situation seems pretty tense again,' said Simón.

Margalit nodded. 'And Gideon right in the thick of it.'

Before I knew it, the conversation had become a fierce argument about the rights and wrongs of the Israel–Palestine conflict. At one point, the discussion turned to military ethics and Margalit mentioned the Israeli Defence Forces' set of ethical principles. I made some sceptical remark about codes of military ethics in general, and she snapped back, 'This is not some academic debating point, David. This is—'

'Okay, time to move on, folks,' said Simón, almost pleading now. 'Time to move on.'

Margalit had turned away from me, a sign that she was not going to engage further. 'I'm sorry for that, Simón,' she said. 'We shouldn't have got into it.'

'Don't apologise, it's a big question.'

'It shouldn't be. Not for a Jew. That's my point.'

There was a difficult silence. Then Alejandra said, 'You might be right, David. To a degree. But the point is, the world is nasty and uncertain. That doesn't mean... Look, you choose your state and your affiliation, and you stick with it. It's not saying everything's fine and ethical and what have you. It's making imperfect choices in an imperfect world. I mean, EuDeFor came out of the impulse to limit violations by individual states, didn't it?'

'That's sort of what I was trying to say, Alejandra. That things aren't black and white.'

'I didn't exactly say that,' she objected.

'And a fine job EuDeFor's making of it,' said Margalit acidly.

I ignored the jibe. 'And anyway, darling,' I said, 'your family always talked about going back to Salonica, not to Israel.'

She in turn ignored my comment. She was looking down, shaking her head, a tight smile. 'When it's a question of the survival of the Jews, things are very black and white, *cariño*. Very black and white.' She made '*cariño*' sound like a whistling bullet rather than a term of endearment.

'You're basically saying I'm a self-hating Jew because I don't unequivocally—'

'Well, if the cap fits...'

I glowered at her, wondering how this could have blown up out of nothing. But I had the sense to bite my tongue for once, and Simón said, 'Hey, people, let's keep things in perspective. We all know married life is a combat zone. Let's have a truce.'

And this time the conversation did move on, to political corruption scandals and whether our then prime minister was the worst or only the second worst since the end of the dictatorship, and the awful rail disaster in Galicia, and whether Shakira and Gerard Piqué would stay together ('Shakira's a *chanteuse*, darling,' said Margalit in a mock-condescending tone), and our kids and their food fads, and their schools; and soon we were all sweetness and light again.

25.

I'm trying to be a Jew in my own manner, even a Catholic one. In the Baltics, I came up against moral dilemmas the whole time. Marce is a simpler beast: whatever helped us – or him – survive was the path to take. But I agonised over doing the right thing, and what the right thing to do was for me, as a would-be Jew. As a human being, for Christ's sake – a *mensch*, as the Ashkenazis would put it. Things became clearer as time went on. Once Kaspars Irbe formed part of our group, a duo became a trio, and there was little question in my mind that we had to protect him as one of our own. Our interpreter, and, as it turned out, saviour. Such an unlikely saviour, though, even after Marce had cut his hair with the cook's knife to get rid of the lice, hacking away at it until he looked like he'd been dragged head first through a threshing machine.

Doing the 'right thing' can lead you to all kinds of dark places. Once, as we lay hidden in a drainage ditch, we witnessed through the field glasses a score of refugees on the road. They were being horribly mistreated by a contingent of militiamen, and we could hear their cries of terror and distress. Irbe persuaded me that we couldn't intervene to help them, despite my impulse to do the 'right thing', something heroic, quixotic even. 'Captain, that militia, if we go near them, they kill everybody. Everybody.' Afterwards, Marce didn't say anything about the incident, but I knew what he was thinking: that getting ourselves and the refugees killed would have been a high price to pay for my guilt at failing to save every member of my crew, among other things. And Margalit, of course, would have scoffed at the idea of my trying to redeem myself for past screw-ups when I should have been focusing on survival.

I lie in bed in Marce's cramped spare room, going over all this. Even now I feel churned up by the refugees' fate. Not to mention all the decisions I took, or failed to take, that might have saved my crew. And the fact that my marriage has slipped, somehow, into its present state of disrepair.

The flat is beginning to stir. Marce's crooning some song or other; not a tango for once. But definitely Argentinian. I can't hear the words, but it's probably something about gauchos. *Here I am, alone in the wide lonely pampas / with only my beautiful lonely mate gourd / and my lonely trusty steed for company.* I exaggerate, but not much. I hear Laura shout in her hoarse morning voice, 'Bloody hell, Marce, why isn't there ever any bloody coffee!' He breaks off his singing to shout back, 'I'm on it!' It's all a welcome distraction. Time for me to stir.

I've not told Marce, but a few days ago I came in to find Laura in her skinny jeans on the sofa. She had her bare feet up on the coffee table and a tumbler of whisky and ice in front of her, alongside a bottle of Johnny Walker three-quarters full. 'Join me,' she said. I told her I had things to do and needed an early night, and she turned her mouth down. '*Aguafiestas!*' Party-pooper. I grinned at her, went through to my bedroom. Caught myself thinking, *nice feet.*

26.

Marce really does adhere to Margalit's 'things are very black-and-white' school of thought. After our escape from a particularly nasty militia, we came across one of the militiamen lying on the verge, badly wounded. It was one of the few times my friendship with Marce was stretched to breaking point, though of course I haven't told van Raalte that.

I knelt to take the man's pulse. I recognised him as part of a group who'd gone through my mobile phone, leering at pictures of Margalit and jeering at one of me wearing a yarmulka at the Passover table. He opened his eyes and whispered, *'Dreckige Jude!'* – filthy Jew (as Marce was quick to translate). I could feel his incomprehensible hatred: he was dying and that was the only thing he wanted to say.

'Let's go. They'll be back and they'll bring dogs.'

'Shoot him!' Marce said.

'What?'

'You heard me. Shoot him.'

I released the safety catch, levelled the pistol. But let it drop again. I'm a military man, I have a code of conduct, even if it isn't black and white, in Margalit's terms. The man shut his eyes, waiting. He murmured something in his poor German, and tried to spit at me.

'Shoot,' Marce said. 'When the others return, which they will, he'll tell them we survived and they'll hunt us down.'

'I won't shoot a man lying injured with his eyes closed.'

'Not to mention him calling you a dirty Jew coward. Fuck's sake, just do it.' Marce looked at me in that sardonic way he has, half-smile, eyebrow lifting. 'Or do I have to do it myself?'

'Feigenbaum—'

He stepped towards the dying guard, gun in hand. 'It's a matter of survival.'

Was he saying I'm not even a proper Jew? Because a proper Jew would do what had to be done?

'It's a war crime,' I said. 'Do you want to be at their level?'

'We're all on the same level, for fuck's sake! What is this, a moral crusade? Or is it that you just don't have the guts?'

'You are not to shoot him, that's an order.'

'You going to stop me?'

'Damn you, Feigenbaum. If you dared to talk to me like that in front of my crew...'

Marce snorted. 'What crew!'

My pulse is racing as I remember the incident. In the end, I didn't shoot the guard, nor did Marce. By the time we'd stopped arguing, he was dead anyway.

Everybody seems to have their own calculus of the price of survival. It reminds me of another heated discussion at Simón and Alejandra's.

Simón asked if we'd seen the film, *Son of Saul*.

'No,' I said.

'Being Jewish is about survival. But more than survival. Even in the extreme situation of a Nazi death camp, this guy's looking for a rabbi to give a dead kid a decent burial at the risk of his own life.'

'But first you have to survive, no?' said Margalit.

'What,' I said, 'law of the jungle? Survival of the fittest? Like, in the camps, you're on a work detail you've lost your cap, you're a dead man when the guards spot you. So you go and nick a cap in the barracks. And condemn someone else to death. Is that what you want?'

'If need be.'

'It's a point of view,' Simón said. 'But a normally moral person would pay a heavy psychological price, later, for doing something like that, don't you think?'

Margalit huffed. Marce, too, would have been derisive, no doubt. They've more in common, those two, than appears on the surface.

I remember on the way home, while we waited at traffic lights, a young guy, west African maybe, rushed forward and began to sponge our windscreen. I waved him away, but Margalit put her hand on my arm. 'Let him. It's a few coins.'

'My windscreen has been cleaned so many times I could eat my dinner off it.'

The lights changed, I handed over a couple of euros, and we drove off again.

'*Gemilut hasidim*,' she said.

Of course she did.

I looked at her out of the corner of my eye. 'You're one of the kindest, most empathetic people I know, my love, and there you are defending extreme positions on survival.'

'Okay, maybe you're right, there's a bit of a contradiction there. But who's always entirely consistent? For me there's so much family history, you know – Salonica, the Holocaust. I mean, you accept your fate, or you resist. I've come down on the side of not going passively to the slaughter. Everything else can have your shades of grey, that's fine.'

I sighed. 'I just don't have the history.'

'What about your mother's history? Talk to her.'

'I will.'

I took one hand off the steering wheel to squeeze her knee. 'I'll try not to wind you up, darling.'

'Same to you,' she said.

As we turned into Filipinas, she lifted my hand to her lips and kissed it, before replacing it on the steering wheel. She leaned across and kissed my cheek. Her black hair tickled my face, and I smelled the warm notes of her perfume. She touched me lightly with her fingertips and let her hand fall to my thigh. Like a casual, accidental gesture that she knew very well would turn me on.

'Take me home, *caballero*,' she said. 'Take me home.'

27.

Margalit has such a good sense of where she's come from, even several generations back. When the kids were still small, 2011 it would have been, she and I went to Salonica. She'd had an invitation to speak at a conference on the Sephardic legacy in Thrace, and was preparing a talk on mutual borrowings of medicinal herbs and spices in Sephardic and Ottoman cultures. Elena agreed to child-mind so that I could go with Margalit.

In the evenings we'd stroll through the old town to the seafront, then go for a dinner of fried fish and garlic and lemon in one of the restaurants looking out over the water, drink white wine, and watch the sun dip below the horizon. This one evening, Margalit was lost in thought.

'The olives are good,' I said.

'Oh. Olives.' She picked up a cocktail stick and put it down again.

'You thinking about your talk, *cariño*?'

'About my family. Strange to think they lived here two or three generations back, walked these streets, breathed the sea air, smelled the rotting fish smell from the harbour.' She wrinkled her nose. 'They had this view.' She pointed out of the window towards the sea. 'Heard the sounds of Greek being spoken – shouted more often than not – alongside Judaeo-Spanish. Your own mother, David, her forebears probably touched down in Salonica somewhere along the line.'

'There's not much left of the community now.'

'Not on the surface. But it's all around us and beneath us. Like at the university.'

The institution where Margalit's conference was being held had expanded onto the site of the old Jewish cemetery after it had been destroyed in the war.

'I'm wondering whether I should say "your august institution, as it happens, is built on the bones of Sephardi victims." Might not go down so well.'

'Say what you feel you have to say.'

I stared out at the mirrored, coppery sea, like a tourist postcard of an Aegean sunset, so different from the wide grey Atlantic swells I knew and loved. 'Does there ever come a point,' I said, 'where you have to let the past rest?'

'Is that a rhetorical question, darling? Or are you saying I should be diplomatic?'

'I don't know, you have to decide.'

Each day, when Margalit was at the conference, I'd walk through the city, breathing in aromatic gusts from the herb market, and the pines in the hills, and the treacly Greek cigarettes. All these smells, so different to those of Madrid, or life on an ocean-going ship of the line. I'd wander back down to the waterfront. On one side of the street, white blocks of apartments, hotels, restaurants. On the other, immediately, without warning, the road's edge and the open waters sparkling in the midday sun. The nearness of the Aegean unsettled me; a call to set sail I couldn't answer.

When Margalit was free, we'd walk the city together. She'd point out the location of the old Jewish quarters and tell me about her family: the ones who'd stayed and died, the ones who'd gone to Spain in the 1920s, those who'd returned to Salonica after the war. A centuries-old community – still speaking the Judaeo-Spanish of the homeland their forebears had left in 1492. Destroyed by the Nazis in a matter of months.

'But there are Jews here again,' she said. 'Not very many. Still, we're tenacious, no?'

On one of our walks we were a few minutes from the port, in a busy street in the centre, when Margalit stopped at a white-painted block with balconies. She said, 'We're going to pay a visit.' She rang the bell, and the faded voice of an old woman said, 'Hello, yes?'

'Is that Señora Roza Ezratti?'

'Yes. Who is this? What do you want?'

'It's Margalit. Margalit Toledano.'

'Who?'

'Toledano. Margalit. Your great-niece. From Madrid.'

'What! From Spain? Of the Spanish Toledanos?'

'I did write, perhaps you didn't...'

'Write? Nobody writes. And the post is shit. At least, I never get any. Come up. Fourth floor, God willing.'

A buzzer sounded and the entrance door clicked open. We took the lift, and a tiny woman met us, in her eighties, curving spine, thinning white hair cut very short, startling pale blue-grey eyes.

Margalit had to stoop to kiss her cheeks. 'I'm sorry, I should have written again. But I didn't know if...'

'What, if I was still alive?' She cackled. 'Well, as you can see, I'm alive, I'm alive!'

'So you're a Toledano, eh?' Roza said when she'd brought us into her apartment. 'You look like a Toledano.'

She spoke a version of Spanish with a distinctive pronunciation. Margalit says it's the influence of Judaeo-Spanish, Ladino. Spanish with a sprinkling of Hebrew and Turkish. Although *judeo-español* has almost died out now in Greece, Roza would have learnt it as a child. We had no trouble understanding each other.

'Yes,' said Margalit. 'A Toledano. From Madrid. My grandfather was Isaac. I'm sorry, we should have phoned first.'

'Isaac. Ah, Isaac. Sit, sit.'

Roza went to make coffee. When she came back she said, 'From Madrid. About time! Sixty-odd years I've waited for one of you *mamzerim* to come and visit!' Her laugh was a dry rattle.

'I know,' Margalit said. 'It's very remiss, auntie.'

'And this is?' Roza said, gesturing towards me.

'David, my partner.'

'Oh, partner, very modern.' She smiled at me. 'So, Margalit, you're one of the Seville nieces?'

'Right. Though I don't know if I am a niece exactly. You were a second cousin of Isaac, weren't you?'

'Oh don't ask me, I could never work these things out. Something like that. Part of the same family anyway. So tell me, how are they all?'

'Isaac's son Alejandro is my father.'

'Still alive?'

'Yes.'

'So how is he?'

'He's okay. Ay, Roza, it's complicated. Things didn't work out in my marriage, so relations are strained.'

'What, your husband beat you? That's normal.' She glanced briefly at me.

'No, not that.'

'What then?'

'You know.'

'No, I don't know, tell me. We're *mishpocheh*, after all.' Roza held up her hands. 'All right, all right, don't tell me.'

Margalit sighed. 'Turns out he's gay. Homosexual.'

'Oh my goodness.'

'Well you did ask. Nothing wrong with being gay, of course. Only, he didn't think to let me know before we got married, I only found out afterwards, and...'

'And marriages are made in bed. Or fail. Eh?'

'You know, it's difficult. My husband, Arturo, wouldn't give me a religious divorce, so in my parents' eyes we're still married. And I'm... I'm a whore, more or less, so I barely see them.'

I didn't expect what happened next: Margalit started to cry. I took her hand and held it.

Roza gazed at me with her intense pale eyes. 'So this is not your husband?'

Margalit shook her head. 'No, *tía*. Well, not in Jewish law. He's my lover.' She grinned through the tears, and moved her hand to the back of my neck and stroked it. 'And the father of my son.'

I liked being called her *amante*.

'You've done very well, I have to say. I wouldn't mind a lover myself.' Roza laughed.

'We have two children, Sarita and Rubencito. The girl I had with Arturo before we separated, Rubén with David. *Mamzerim*, I guess you could call them!'

'Young people today!'

Margalit brought out her phone and showed her aunt photographs of the kids, and Roza murmured, '*Qué bonitos, ay, qué bonitos!* Lovely. The little one looks like his father.'

I listened to them talking about family. About the sweet fritters Margalit's grandmother used to make, about her grandfather Isaac singing Ladino songs to her when she was a girl.

'There was one especially I loved, lilting, like a lullaby. I can't remember all the words.' Margalit took her aunt's hands and started to hum in her tuneful high, girlish voice. The melody was beautiful, wistful. She'd never sung it to me.

Roza smiled. '*Arvoles yoran por yuvias*. Trees cry for rain.'

'Yes, that's the one.'

Roza made no attempt to sing, but she recited in a sort of chant, '*Trees cry for rain / And mountains for the breeze. / So my eyes weep / For you, my beloved. / In a strange land / I am going to die*. But my dear, it was the song the deportees sang as they left Salonica on the Nazi trains.'

'Yes, exactly. Except in the last verse, they sang "In *Polish lands* I am going to die." So they must have known what was going to happen to them in Auschwitz.'

'Oh, they knew,' said Roza. 'We all knew.'

She offered us more pastry. 'So Isaac used to sing that to you?'

'Yes.'

'I shouldn't be saying this, but I was so in love with your grandfather. You know, in a cousinly sort of way.' She wobbled her head from side to side, evaluating her own statement. 'I don't know, maybe not so cousinly! Ha, Isaac, what a handsome boy. Much older than me, I was hardly into my teens when the Germans arrived. I don't think he even noticed me among all the cousins and aunts. Oh my goodness, Isaac Toledano.' Roza's eyes disappeared behind the papery folds of her lids. 'I came back to Salonica after the war, got married, had children. But it was different, of course. And always, this pain in your guts, after what happened. With what's happening now. You know these New Day types—'

'Golden Dawn?' I suggested.

'Oh, whatever they call themselves. They still want to get rid of the Jews, so my son tells me. Oh *Dios mío*. So what's the point? My son lives in Athens. I'm alone and a prisoner in my own home.'

Margalit took her hand and stroked it. 'Tell me about the Germans, *tía*, how did you manage to get out?'

'Oh, you don't want to know about that, it's ancient history.'

I said, 'Actually she's a historian. She does like to hear these things.'

'David—' said Margalit.

'A historian? You don't want to talk to me then, you want to go to the archives.'

'But history is also talking to people who were there.'

'So I'm history am I?' Roza laughed again, slapping at her niece's hand.

'You know what I mean. I just thought, you know, most people didn't get out.'

'We were lucky. In life, luck has so much to do with it.' She picked absently at the fabric of her sleeve. 'Yes, we had luck, *mami* and I. The trains were already taking the Jews to Poland, to Auschwitz as we learned after the war. Hardly any came back.'

Margalit said, 'But you managed to avoid the trains?'

'We were saved by the Spanish consul here, I can't remember his name. Good-looking man, hair carefully combed back, neat moustache. Apparently there was a Spanish law...'

'That's right,' said Margalit, 'it was the decree of 1924—'

'Yes, dear, I'm sure you know the ins-and-outs. But it was all very complicated for us. We had to wait a long time, they put us on a train to Athens, more waiting, and in the end we got to Belgium and then Spain. I can't remember the details, I must have been twelve or thirteen, we were exhausted, and of course my father wasn't with us and we didn't ever see him again. My mother's heart was broken and she died not long after we got to Spain. I went back to Salonica after the war, because it was what I knew, and where my sister Ana was. She'd been deported and had survived Auschwitz, though when she came back she was never the same, of course.'

'And my grandfather Isaac, *tía*?'

'Ah, Isaac!' said Roza. 'He was still a teenager when the Germans arrived, but he came back to visit me a few years after the war. I was into my twenties and pretty good-looking, you know.'

'I bet you were.'

'I was free, my parents were dead. Ha, those days! I just sat looking at him, lured him in with my gaze! He had those thick black sideburns, brought out his burning eyes, oh my goodness. And we had a brief affair, it's true. He was a lot older, of course. People were very free for a short period, all the old rules collapsed. He went back to Seville, got married, broke my heart. And I met my husband, and life became... normal.' She tried to laugh but trailed off, eyes wide and looking down at the past. She roused herself. 'Have more coffee. And cake.'

She held out a plate of sweet, date-filled balls of dough. I could smell the rosewater as I bit into one.

She said, 'I don't know why I'm telling you all this. I suppose it's not having anyone to talk to.'

'It's lovely to hear you talk, *tía*. But tell me, how did Isaac survive the Germans? That's rather important for me being alive at all!'

'With luck. And courage. He had a good friend who was Greek, whose father was a policeman, and with his help he escaped to Athens. Then he went to fight with the *andartes*, in the hills. That's how he survived.'

'I remember saying to him, "And, grandpa, did you ever *kill* a man?" And he'd go, "Many! With these hands!" I can picture him, holding up his big wide hands, and I could easily imagine him killing a man with them.'

Roza said, 'He could never understand why they didn't take any notice of the warning signs and try to get away. We all knew what was happening. We were being thrown out of our own houses. Our belongings stolen. The cemetery smashed up. Why would we believe them when they said we'd have a new life in Poland? Isaac said to me after the war, "Roza, I knew there were only two paths: resignation or resistance. I chose resistance." Which sounds a bit pompous, I know. But the way he said it…!'

'He used to say that to me, too.'

Roza's eyes glinted and she gave another chesty laugh. 'This is what happens when things get stirred up, it's like there's no stable ground any more.'

She began to weep.

Margalit said gently, '*Tía*, why are you crying?'

'Because when you've gone, I shall just feel more lonely.' She tried to smile and wiped her eyes with her fingers. 'Forgive me, I'm just a silly old woman stuck at home on my own, with my stupid memories.'

28.

I've come to the Chamberí flat today to fetch some more clothes. Margalit's in. We exchange a couple of polite sentences. As I turn to leave, I notice a pile of identical paperbacks on the sideboard by the door: *Los Sefardíes en el mundo*. By Margalit Toledano, published by Marcial Pons Historia.

'It's published?'

'Yes. Last week, launch party. Told you umpteen times.'

'I'm sorry. Congratulations. Did it go okay?'

'Yes, it was fine.' She folds her arms.

I stand awkwardly for a few moments, waiting for her. But she doesn't move.

'Okay,' I say, 'I'll see you in a few days.'

'I expect so.'

I'm going out the door when she calls me back.

'David, I should let you know – I'm thinking about Israel.'

'Israel? What do you mean? Thinking what, exactly?'

'*Aliyah*. Emigrating. For Sara and Rubén's sake, for the future.'

'You're not serious? You can't do that. Where do I figure in your—'

'I've relatives near Haifa. There are jobs. Good schools.'

'I know things have been difficult between us, but that's completely ridiculous. Why is this the first I've heard about it? Why haven't you discussed it?'

She's always going on about *Sefarad*, the mythical place, the garden of Eden, blah-blah. About her forebears being expelled from it in 1492. And how they've been dreaming about it ever since. She's back here in Spain, in *Sefarad*, and she's still not satisfied.

'Israel isn't a safe place, for God's sake,' I say. 'It's a war zone. Just look at—'

'Madrid isn't secure. Atocha bombings. Hate crimes. I'd feel less insecure among my own people.'

'And where do I fit in, Margalit? Where do I fit in?'

She looks at me without saying anything.

'You've been to Israel,' I say. 'You told me you hated it. All the noise, everybody so brash and in your face. Everything you can't stand.'

'Yes, but that was different.'

'Not to mention Sephardi Jews being pretty downtrodden there, so you said.'

'Less than they were. Much less.'

'I'm trying to work things out, and you want to emigrate to Israel. I really don't get it.'

Sara comes into the room. 'What are you two arguing about?' There's a note of anxiety mixed in with the insolence.

'Does she know about this?' I ask.

Sara looks at me with half-opened mouth, gives a scornful little snigger, and walks through to the kitchen.

Margalit's announcement has floored me. I swing between confusion and anger as I take the metro back to Marce's flat with my bag of clothes. How serious is she?

I'm standing in the middle of the sitting room, like I've forgotten where I'm supposed to be. The door to the second bedroom opens. Laura emerges and weaves her way through the piles of Marce's books and cardboard boxes. He lived here with Laura at first, but they broke up and she moved out. Then she moved back in again. I never did understand his 'arrangements'.

'*Hola, majo*,' she calls. 'Is he in?'

'I don't know,' I say.

She blows me a kiss. 'Sorry, haven't got time to stop. See you later,' and she's out the door.

Marce hasn't gone out. I now hear him loading the plates into the dishwasher. He's started singing a Gardel tango in his tuneful tenor voice. He comes into the living room with a couple of beers and, still singing, throws me a can. He's a useful distraction from my anxious thoughts.

The song is something about still having affection for a woman he once loved. I often heard him hum it when we bedded down for the night on our trek, and immediately I'm back in those cold rotting barns with their rusting scythes and old bicycles and stink of ammonia. I try to shut out the images. I want to tell him to stop singing, but it's his flat.

'Hello, Marce.'

'Hello, have you seen Laura?'

'She went out.'

He plonks himself down on the sofa.

'What's the attraction? The whole Argentinian thing, *che*. The tango, the *milongas*, the pictures on the wall.'

He shrugs. 'It's where my parents were from. My heritage, isn't it.'

'But you've never been. And if you had, the pampas would hardly be your stamping ground.'

'So how much do you know about your "heritage"?'

'More than I did.'

He takes a moment to think.

'Argentina, tango, I don't know. All the words about pain and regret, lost love, yearning. Gardel, that voice, that crackle on the recordings, it gets to me, it's so... soulful.'

'*Soulful?*'

'Yes. Dad used to play them on his old record player until they were more crackle than song.' He rubs at his buzzcut hair with the flat of his hand. 'I suppose wanting something less humdrum. Something more glamorous, more adventurous. With more romance, if that's the word. Shit, what the hell am I on about!'

'Romantic? You? Come on, Marce, man.'

'I don't mean romantic like in fairy tales, like happy ever after. Not like you, David. Not like you and your Margalit.' He holds up his hand, placatory, before I can take offence. 'Sorry, I know it's not looking so happy-ever-after currently. You know what I mean. Something beyond ourselves.'

'You turning religious? Lord help us.'

'Fuck, no. I mean a mood, evocative of something else. Lights low, clink of beer bottles, popular music – music that loads your memories. Smell of cheap cigarettes, cheap scent on a woman dancing. Late night smells. Hmm. I had this idea once, of a machine, like a DVD player but for smells. You could record them, then years later play them, and be plunged backwards in time. To a bar, to a woman you loved for a while. To... I don't know. It makes me think of my father, I suppose.'

'Last thing I'd want to do is go back to the smells of my childhood.'

'Such as?'

'Oh, I don't know. The stuffy smell of our living room, smell of mothballs around my adoptive mother. My father's breath after one of his cigars. It's the last thing I'd want.'

'The smell of Margalit?'

He's caught me unawares. Even if she and the kids don't go to Israel, what does our future hold? I sit here now, forgetting about Marce for a moment, agonising about her being surrounded by charismatic, accomplished, literary men who write or publish books. Some of them even Jewish. Has she been wined and dined? Seduced? By an Israeli, maybe? *Ay*, Margalit, Margalit.

Marce's voice becomes insistent. 'David? You okay?'

'Uh?'

'I didn't mean to touch a sensitive spot.'

'No problem, Marce, forget it.'

We open more beer, turn on the evening news bulletin. Russia has seized Ukrainian naval vessels in the Sea of Azov.

'All quiet on the eastern front,' says Marce.

'This could get tense, no? What will EuDeFor do?'

'Send a rust bucket of a tugboat out of Toulon. Lucky the Pandora already went down, or they'd be sending us.'

I try to smile, but I have a sour, panicky sensation in my stomach.

We talk about going to a local bar later. At which point Laura returns. She winks at Marce, waves at me, calls out, *'Hola, cabrones!'* and goes to her room.

I murmur, 'Not prying or anything, but you and Laura...?'

Laura's as skinny and sardonic as Marce. Attractive in a fizzing, tactile sort of way. She's got his same manner of looking at the world with cynical amusement. Maybe that's because they've lived together for so long. They sleep in separate rooms, but more than once I've heard comings and goings in the night, noisy orgasms.

'What?' says Marce with amused fake innocence.

'You know.'

'Why? You interested? She's pretty much free as far as I know.'

I say, 'I'm a married man, Feigenbaum.'

'Being married is a continuum.'

'So I see.'

'But if you're more at the married end of being married, why are you here, and not in Chamberí with your family?'

'Good question. I'm working on it.' I take a swig of beer. 'But you and Laura, you know...?'

'What? Do we screw? Occasionally. It's a friendly arrangement, doesn't mean anything. Peaceful coexistence, if you like.'

'*Ay*, Feigenbaum, Feigenbaum.'

He gazes at me with that wry smile. He sees me before I see myself.

29.

The days pass. I've been at Marce's place for a couple of weeks; it seems longer. We're into December and the weather's misty, and it's cold at night. But at least there's some sunshine after the autumn gloom. I've come to the Chamberí flat to see Rubén this morning. Margalit is busying herself around the place. Her greeting is matter-of-fact, neutral. She says nothing about Israel, and I don't ask.

'He's waiting for you in the other room.'

Rubencito is in one of his chattier moods, which basically means pestering me for more details of the sinking, and of my odyssey across the Baltic badlands. Especially escaping from the Mitsubishi Warriors – the very name has him wide-eyed at the notion that utility vehicles are *warriors*. He's fascinated that our militia captors used zip ties to handcuff us. He also wants to know what we ate on the move; how we kept ourselves clean when we did our business; whether we were tortured and, if so, how; what guns we had; what guns *they* had; how far we hiked; whether we got blisters. No amount of detail is enough.

As usual, I try to fob him off with a sanitised, bare-bones version. As quickly as I can, I turn the conversation to his schoolwork, how he's doing in class, his friends. He gives monosyllabic answers then uses his assignments as an excuse to slink off to his room – I suspect to play on his games console.

Margalit comes through from the kitchen. 'David, can't you see he really wants to talk about what happened to you?'

'I've told him quite a bit.'

'He needs more. Talk about it seriously with him. Not like you're reading from the captain's log, for heaven's sake! Because he feels he's losing you.' She takes a breath and says, more calmly, 'You know, he was terrified. He thought you were dead. We all did. He's traumatised, and he needs to work through it. Make it real for him, otherwise you're a sort of ghost. His imagination will take over, and it will be harder for him to make sense of it all.'

'He won't want to hear the detail, it's too gruesome and—'

'You underestimate his resilience. You're fobbing him off and he knows it. Just talk to him.'

'Okay. Okay.'

I have a sudden brainwave, and go down the corridor to Rubén's room. He has headphones on.

'Rubén, you asked about zip ties.'

I perch on the edge of his bed. He takes the headphones off.

'Zip ties.' I hold my wrists together. 'Are there any in the house?'

'I don't know, Mum might have some for staking the plants on the balcony. Why?'

I go in search of ties. Margalit finds some in a kitchen drawer. 'What's this about? Don't use them all.'

I return to Rubén's bedroom.

'Bind my wrists,' I say.

He does so.

'Tighter.' I take the loose end between my teeth and pull as hard as I can.

'I thought you were trying to get out of them.'

'Just watch.'

I go down on one knee, bring my arms as high into the air as I can and crash them down so the centre of the tie hits my raised knee. The tie splits.

'What! Wait, how…? That's pretty cool. Let me try.'

He jumps up from the bed and I secure him in his own set of ties. He attempts two or three times to break them, without success. I cut him loose with a pair of scissors.

'I'm going to practise,' he says. 'There must be a knack to it.'

'Good idea, practice is what you need. Don't use them all.'

'So that's how you escaped from the Mitsubishi Warriors?'

'Yes. Marce knows about these things, escape techniques.'

'Would he give me a demo, d'you reckon?'

'I'm sure he would. We'll get you round to his place.'

He makes his fingers into a pistol. 'I'm holding you to that, *papi*.' His expression goes serious. 'Dad?'

'Yes?'

'Did they hurt you? The militias, I mean.'

I lie. 'Oof, it was only like a really bad tackle in a game of football.'

'Hmm,' he says, sceptically. 'Were you scared?'

I take in a long breath. 'Yes, *hijo*, I was scared. Sometimes very scared.'

'Like when the ship went down?'

'Of course.'

'And when the militias captured you, and when they...?'

'Yes, Rubén, yes.'

'Did you pray?'

'What, *"Hail, Mary, full of grace, the Lord is with thee, blessed is the fruit of thy womb, Jesus..."*?'

'Dad!'

'No, I didn't pray. Would you have prayed?'

He considers this for a moment and says, 'Hmm. You don't really know until you're in that situation, do you.'

'Quite.'

'Did you think you were going to die?'

I hesitate again, staring into space.

'Dad? Did you?'

'Yes, my lovely boy, I did think I was going to die.'

'Do you still think about it?'

I nod. 'Yes. I mean, you would think about it, wouldn't you.'

'I kind of know what you mean.'

Then, to my consternation, this wan, rather frail and withdrawn boy grins at me, reaches out, pats my back and gives me a hug, his chin against my shoulder, and I realise how damaged and weak I've become, rusted away beneath the steel carapace.

'But you didn't die, *papi*, and you did make it back, so that's all good.'

I put my arm round him and hold him tight.

As I leave, Margalit gives me just the hint of a smile, and the slightest lift of her eyebrows.

I get back to Marce's with a bag of groceries. He comes in from wherever he's been, cheerful as usual.

'Hello, *hermano*, how are we doing?'

'Average.'

'Sounds pretty upbeat coming from you.'

'Got some cutlets and fruit, by the way, they're in the fridge.'

'Great.'

'Went to see Rubén this morning. He'd love to speak to you about escape techniques and survival.'

'Happy to. Did you see the Kiel hearings have been postponed again, to the New Year?'

'Yes. For "operational reasons". Van Raalte told me.'

'So you can relax on the preparation.'

'I'm not sure we can. The better prepared we are—'

'What, you want to do some kind of role play? Sure. I can be the aggressive EuDeFor counsel trying to trick you into contradicting yourself.'

'Can we take this seriously for once, Marce? It's our careers at stake.'

'I know, David. But we've been over it a dozen times. If you want to write a "what I did in the Baltic" memoir, go ahead.' He considers me for a moment. 'And what about Margalit?'

'Not much to report.'

'Not that I'm hassling, or anything.'

'Thanks,' I say. But I know he won't want me here forever. And of course I don't wish to be here for a minute longer than is necessary.

30.

Just when there was a faint flicker of hope, I've gone and sabotaged myself. The psychoanalysts would have a field day.

Last night. I just wish I could erase it. Press delete.

Marce was out on the tiles, and I shared a couple of bottles of wine with Laura. She lit a joint, which I declined to share, and chain-drank. I don't know why I didn't just stop after a glass or three, but I kept pace with her.

'I'm still in love with Marce, you know. Utter bastard that he is.' Her voice was husky from the tobacco and booze.

'In love with him? I'm not sure he sees it like that.'

'He's an idiot. He doesn't understand women.'

I laughed. 'Neither do I.'

She gave me a look, as if to say, *I take that for granted.* 'If he wasn't such a bastard, he wouldn't let me stay here.'

'If he didn't let you stay here, you'd think he was even more of a bastard.'

'True, oh wise one.' She took a swig of wine. 'Hey, I've got the munchies.'

Then she told me I had nice shoulders and next thing I knew we were kissing. I pulled away and stammered, 'I'm sorry, I can't—'

'I know, I know, you're spoken for, don't tell me. I'm not asking you to marry me for fuck's sake.'

And we had sex in the double bedroom, urgent, enjoyable, in the moment.

Afterwards, I fell asleep like I'd been poleaxed. Woke in the night to the sound of the doorknob squeaking. Marce tiptoeing into the room. He saw me, stopped for a moment, no doubt perplexed at the unexpected sight of me in his bed. He raised a hand. 'Sorry,' he whispered, 'No, no, don't get up for me, I'll sleep in the other room!'

'Sorry,' I whispered back.

'Don't be! See you in the morning.'

I drifted back to sleep and half-woke, felt the brush of Laura's body. She began to caress my chest, my arms. It took me a moment to work out where I was, and with whom. When I did realise, I felt physically sick. I edged away from her. She sighed, as if in disappointment, and fell straight back to sleep. I eased out of bed and went through to the sofa in the lounge.

Couldn't sleep, of course. I lay there, coming up with all sorts of worthless self-justifications: *Margalit's cold, she's cutting herself off from me, she's rejecting me, when was the last time we made love? Don't even remember. She's rejecting my career and life choices, not even a personal invite to her book launch. She's planning to take the kids and shoot off to Israel.* Nothing halted the tide of shame and self-disgust.

And this morning comes the fear: for the future of our marriage, for the future of my brilliant career. I have endless echoing questions about who I am and where I'm going in my life – my stupid fucking self-sabotaging life. Everything coming together in my mind, a perfect storm. I catch myself thinking, *All that for a quick shag with a budding alcoholic.* I rebuke myself: unworthy of me to be contemptuous of Laura. But I feel angry with her, angry with Margalit, angry with my adoptive parents and my real mother. Angry with me.

31.

I turn on my mobile and find a message from Margalit: *Ring me.* I call her and she tells me a friend of Elena's phoned to say she's in hospital. I'm relieved to have a pretext to get out of the flat, away from the scene of the crime, as it were. I throw on some clothes and take a cab to the hospital. My brain's scrambled, I'm still hungover.

In the oncology ward Elena is dozing fitfully amid all the tubes and wires. Her face is bloated from the steroids. She wakes, and smiles at me. 'Thanks for coming.'

I feel I don't deserve her smile. 'You don't have to thank me, for goodness' sake. How are you doing?'

'Oh, fine in the circumstances. But how are *you*? You look awful, frankly.'

'I'm fine,' I mutter. If she wasn't looking so frail, I'd have been tempted to confess my *peccadillo*, get it off my chest.

She coughs. 'They're trying to adjust my medication, and I may have a blockage they'll need to clear. You don't want to know the details.'

'How long are you in for?'

'You tell me!' She winces. 'But what's going on with you? How's the family?'

'I'm, you know, waiting for the inquiry. I'll have to go to Kiel, as a witness. In January.'

'Germany?'

'Afraid so. It's where their headquarters are.'

'It'll be good to get it out of the way and get on with your life. Waiting around must be demoralising.'

'I worry I'll be out of the country...'

'What, when I pop my clogs?'

'I wasn't going to put it like that.'

'Ach, don't worry yourself. Life goes on.' She presses my hand. 'But you dodged my question: what about the family? Things still not so good with Margalit?'

'Could be better.'

'You're not still at Marce's, are you?'

Elena likes Marce but thinks he's 'disreputable', which I suppose he is, and an accomplice in my failure to confront my marital problems.

'It's only very temporary,' I say.

'David, promise me you'll sort it out.' She coughs, and puts her fist to her mouth. I pass her a glass of water.

'I promise.'

On the way back, I stop at the Chamberí flat. Margalit opens the door.

'I just wanted to say many congratulations for the book, I was caught by surprise the other day.'

'Thank you. Have you been to see your mother?'

'I've just come from the clinic. She's not great, it's a question of dealing with the problem and getting her back home.'

'I'll pop in this afternoon.'

'That would be kind.'

'It's what you do.'

'I know.'

'Wait a moment.' She goes to pick up a couple of stapled sheets of paper from the living room.

'What's this?'

'The *kaddish*. The prayer you'll have to say at the funeral.'

'What? She's not dead yet.'

'I'm being practical. So should you be. Prepare. And remember, no flowers.'

'I'm not about to start reciting—'

'You're her closest living relative. You have to. It's how things are done. It's how Jews go to their resting place: with the *kaddish*. Don't worry, I've transliterated it. Even you could read it.'

As an afterthought, she adds, 'Oh, by the way, there's an invitation.' She points to a card stuck in the mirror above the sideboard in the hall. It reads, *Arturo Pérez Greco and Julián Sanz García request the pleasure of your company at their wedding.*

'A *gay* wedding? Who the hell is this?'

'Arturo, my ex-husband.'

'And he invites his estranged ex-wife? That's weird.'

'He's found his half orange, he's feeling magnanimous. I don't expect I'll be going, but you might like to.'

'Oh sure!'

'Sarita's very excited.'

I huff, fold the *kaddish* sheets and put them in the pocket of my jacket.

'And Israel? Emigrating?'

'We're looking into it.'

'But I want us to be able to talk about things. I don't want us just to—'

'You've shown so little inclination to talk about things, David, and God knows I've given you plenty of opportunities. I need more than just your expressions of intent.'

'Please, my love...'

'For God's sake, you smell of another woman. Didn't you even shower before going to see your mother?'

She turns her back and walks through to the kitchen.

32.

Seeing Elena in that state yesterday has made me think I should drop in on Rocío. *Just do it now*, I tell myself. It's probably also making amends, a kind of penance – relieving my horrible feelings of guilt. So I take the metro to Goya and walk along to calle Alcántara. The weather has turned chilly.

My adoptive mother is getting on a bit, late seventies, living in the same flat as always. She's frail but uncomplaining. The old place has seemed brighter since Rafael died, less rigidly ordered. With her circle of Catholic women friends and her church-going and charity work, Rocío keeps herself busy.

Every time I go, I'm pitched back to childhood, though the neighbourhood has changed a lot since I lived there. The blocks of flats all have air conditioning units now, but back in the eighties, I remember, Rocío would just get the maid to close all the shutters and wet the marble and parquet flooring with a mop to keep the summer heat at bay.

I visited her when I first got back from the Baltics. She embraced me and didn't let me go for ages, trying not to let me see her crying into my shoulder, which I found slightly uncomfortable. She stroked my hair and face, and mumbled about how she thought I'd died. 'No, Rocío, I didn't die, and here I am.' 'Thank God, thank God, thank God!' More tears. Before I left for my Baltic posting, I used to visit her every couple of months. Sometimes I'd take Rubén. She was always delighted to see us. She'd make a fuss of him, offer him slices of pastry, slip him a twenty-euro note. He'd be his normal reserved self, of course.

Today, she makes coffee, too weak as usual, serves it in her best bone china. The dining room is stuffy, the central heating turned up too high. When she asks about the family I'm evasive, and she doesn't press me. I do tell her about Elena's health, though, and she's sympathetic.

'Oh, *Dios mío*, what a tragedy! I'm so sorry, David, *querido*, so sorry for her, poor woman.'

Perhaps it makes her think about her own role as a mother, because she starts to reminisce.

'Just the other day I was thinking about when you were a little boy and – do you remember? – we used to go down to that pedestrian square with the benches, you and me and sometimes Pilar who was your childminder. You know where I mean?

Just behind El Corte Inglés – they've spruced it up since then.'

'And you used to buy me a packet of sunflower seeds from the old man at his little stall. He had that funny cloudy eye I didn't like.'

'Sunflower seeds, yes. We'd walk round a few times and walk home again. It was nice to get out of the flat, especially on the warm summer evenings.'

I remember kids running about and dusk coming on, the greasy sweet smell of churros, birdsong, the bats darting in and out of the trees.

'You used to tell me off for spitting out the shells, seeing how far I could get them.'

'Well, you did make a performance of it.'

'You remember the bats?'

'Oh yes, always bats, and only a stone's throw from the main road. Swifts, too.'

We'd stop off at El Corte Inglés on the way home and go down the escalator to the food hall where Rocío would take her ticket and wait patiently at the cooked meat counter until her number clicked up on the machine, which I used to watch in fascination. When her turn came she'd wave her ticket like a lottery winner and call out, *'Aquí, aquí,'* in case the attendant behind the counter should miss her and move on, and she'd buy 100 grammes of *jamón de jabugo*. I loved watching the man wield his narrow knife and carve the ham so thinly off the leg, with such nonchalance, and if he went slightly over weight Rocío would say, 'Too much, take a slice off,' and he'd comply with a swishing motion, without saying a word or looking at her, and he'd say, 'Anything else, *señora*?' and she'd always say, 'Nothing else.'

'Sometimes,' I say, 'you used to buy some ham on the way back, you remember?'

'That's right. Your father would have had a fit if he'd known how much a few slices cost. But he never did any shopping so he never knew, and he didn't ask.'

'You used to tell me the pigs had a good life and a diet of acorns in the woods.'

'Did I?'

'I had an image of all these little black pigs rootling for their fodder under the oak trees. And the smells of that cold meats counter, for me as a little boy – paradise.'

Rocío smiles. She strokes my hand. 'It seems like only yesterday, you know.' And I see that those little outings were the highlight of her day, a relief and refuge for her as they were for me. When I leave, she hugs me close.

As I walk back in the direction of the metro station, I sense that I don't have to wipe away my childhood, my upbringing, my memories; that I should just try to accept they're part of who I am, alongside the newer, Jewish, layer. And learn to integrate the different strata.

My thoughts, of course, keep getting spiked by the intrusion of the Laura thing. The guilt is a tonne weight, a physical entity that makes my shoulders sag and slump. As I pass the church of San Miguel y San Benito, I stop, unpremeditated, taken with the idea that I should go in and confess: relieve myself of a few kilos of the guilt. I even glance at the timetable on the noticeboard outside. *Confessions: Make a request from half an hour before the starting time of each mass.*

What deters me is the thought of having to tell the priest that it's been twenty-something years since I last confessed, and that, yes, I have abandoned the faith. Not to mention hearing Marce's caustic voice in my head: *Man, you're in a worse way than I thought,* joder! *Is it a Jew? Is it a Catholic? No! It's Captain Aguilera! You'd be better off talking to a shrink than a priest.* Et cetera. I walk on.

33.

Today, finally, Marce and I have flown to Hamburg and taken the train to Kiel to give our evidence to the inquiry into the Pandora's demise.

I'm not looking forward to the proceedings, having just spent a miserable, preoccupied Christmas and New Year at Marce's flat. He was off with a woman 'friend' who has a country place near Talavera de la Reina, so I was on my own most of the time. Laura was away too, thank God. I spoke to her briefly before she left. The first time I'd seen her since our encounter. I'd been dreading the moment.

She smiled and said, 'Hi there.'

I said, 'Look, about the other night...'

'What about it?'

'I'm sorry, it shouldn't have happened.'

'Lots of things shouldn't happen but do. They're often the best things, no?'

'I'm serious. It was crazy. It can't happen again.'

'Who says it's going to? Look, *mi capitán*, as far as I'm concerned, nothing happened, okay?' She gave a mock salute. 'Or if it did, it's water under the bridge.'

She peered at my no doubt agonised face. 'I promise I won't pounce on you, if that's what you're worried about. We're *cool*, okay.'

'But—'

'No buts. I know you're trying to get back with your wife.' She folded her hands in front of her and said, in a bright, soothing voice, eyes wide, as if addressing an anxious child, 'Are we happier now?'

I don't know if I can trust her, or if I can trust myself. For it to happen once is one time too many. I don't feel happier, I feel miserable.

Marce seemed on edge when I saw him. 'Well, yes, maybe it wasn't the smartest move on your part, David.'

'I know.'

'I mean, come on, man, she is my ex-wife...' There was an unaccustomed edge to his voice. 'Not to mention that it'll fuck up your chances with Margalit.'

'I know, I know. I've no idea what made me... It was utterly stupid. A moment of madness. Unforgivable. I'm sorry, Marce, truly.'

I ought to have sensed ages ago that Marce was more invested in his relationship with Laura than I'd realised. Maybe more than he'd realised.

But then he shrugged and said, not altogether convincingly, 'No skin off my nose, *hermano*. In fact it might help cut the ties. She's a bit, you know...'

'In love with you still?'

'Let's just say I'm her drug of choice.'

'And you, Marce?'

'It's not a problem, honestly.'

'So you and me?'

'It's okay, we're cool.'

Cool. He and Laura even use the same expressions.

I haven't spoken to Margalit again about it. There's nothing to be said. I went to see her and the kids over the holiday, to give them their Hanukkah-stroke-Christmas presents, and the atmosphere was, unsurprisingly, strained.

I'd made an effort for Sara, nipping into Fnac and asking one of the employees for advice on women novelists. She handed me something by Sara Mesa. I barely gave the cover blurb a glance; the coincidence of names was enough for me to ask the woman to gift-wrap it. She gave me a knowing look. 'It's, you know, dark, edgy... bit erotic.' Erotic. Oh dear. It was too late, she'd already wrapped it. 'You've read it?' I said. She chuckled. 'Lots of silk underwear, if you get my meaning.' It occurred to me as I left the store that my stepdaughter would prefer a Zara gift card or something.

When I'd got to the flat to deliver the presents, Margalit had been looking up Kiel on the internet, which at least suggested she was taking an interest. 'It has all the charm you'd expect of a world-class shipbuilding and maritime transport hub,' she said.

But I'm not here for its charms, and I have an inquiry to get through. As van Raalte says, I'm not on trial, but my reputation's at stake.

EuDeFor's main offices are in an austere grey building on a windy artificial peninsula on the outskirts of Kiel, amid hectares of sidings, concrete aprons, warehouses. The Baltic is grey and choppy, and sea and sky merge in the middle distance. Somewhere out there is Denmark. Marce and I eat and sleep at headquarters, each to our own single room, sparsely furnished like a monk's cell, no outside contact. Each morning we're collected by an adjutant and taken to a meeting room with an oversized light-wood desk where, for hours at a time, we're interviewed by a panel of EuDeFor worthies – three unsmiling men in grey suits and one unsmiling woman, together with a stenographer. The woman is the chair of the panel, a retired rear-admiral, German, with a lean face and narrow-set eyes.

For the first day or two, it has been more like an inquisition. They're aware of my blemished record. Although the inquiry is about establishing facts rather than apportioning blame, I've still felt I have to prove my innocence.

Talking through the events leading up to the disabling of the Pandora and my giving the order to abandon ship, everything seems almost intolerably vivid. A couple of times I have to halt my testimony to collect myself, and the chair has said, 'Take the time you need, Captain.' I'm staring at the yellow needle on the rudder-angle indicator that's refusing to budge from six degrees to starboard, and aware of Feigenbaum's contemptuous smile at the intractability of the equipment on which our lives depend. I see the taut faces of the crew on the bridge, knowing now that many of them – my colleagues, my comrades, some of them my friends – are dead. That peculiar physical sensation, like lead in the stomach, of accepting that in this crisis I'm supremely responsible and, more than ever, must make the right calls, be a leader. And always, that relentless roar and slap of the wind, so loud you can't hear yourself think.

'You weren't there,' I say at one point. 'You have no idea what it's like to be faced with critical decisions coming at you faster than you can process them.' Van Raalte, in attendance, glances at me, uncomfortable at my outburst.

Marce has corroborated the details about the storm and the catastrophic equipment failure and the order to abandon ship. 'I told the bastards that your leadership was exemplary all the way through,' says

Marce on day two, once we're clear of the building. 'That distortion of the facts must be worth at least a beer or two.'

'Agreed,' I say.

The inquiry wants chapter and verse on the aftermath of the sinking. How many crew survived? What did I do to save them? Why couldn't I have done more? Did I leave location markers for any of the deaths, or have any other proof of my account? Where are the naval service tags of those who didn't survive? Why didn't I intervene to try to save the crew in the second lifeboat when they were captured by the militia? And wasn't it a strange coincidence, someone asks, in that infuriatingly neutral tone of voice that inquiry members adopt, that I just happened upon the second lifeboat? 'Coincidence?' I say. 'No, it's not,' – and I can't keep the spikiness out of my voice, despite van Raalte's warning look – 'when you consider you're heading north on a narrow sand spit for forty, fifty kilometres, always within shouting distance of the shore, so no, it's more probable than not that if the craft is there, you will stumble on it. And as for rescuing my crew members, what do people expect? That I shout *Geronimo!* and charge a score of heavily armed militiamen with my service pistol?' Van Raalte turns red and dabs his shiny forehead with a handkerchief. 'Okay,' says the chair, briskly emollient, 'let's return to the Russians.

And the Russian-linked militias. What can you tell us about them?'

'The Russians,' I say, 'were certainly making incursions deep into the Baltic states. Sometimes regular troops, alongside local pro-Moscow militias, sometimes irregulars with no insignia. It's *Maskirovka*: dissembling and deceit. Saying to the world there are no Russian troops or weapons here, what you saw must be agitators, false-flag operatives, trying to damage Russia.'

After a while, the tone of the questioning mellows. They ask me how Feigenbaum and I escaped after being taken captive by the militias. They even nod and smile as I recount the events. Perhaps Marce has told them, with suitable dramatic flourishes, of my role in the escape from the Warriors and in bringing him and Irbe to safety. And, of course, about the zip ties.

It's day three and the panel interviews the two of us together. We take it as a sign that the intense questioning phase is over. I ask about other EuDeFor groups stranded in the Baltics, and the rest of our crew. Some were killed, we're told; others are being held prisoner, for exchange or ransom, it's assumed. A good few are unaccounted for.

Finally the session concludes.

'Is that it?' asks Marce. 'We're free to go?'

'Yes of course,' says the chair. 'Did you expect to be hauled down to the cells, rendered to the International Criminal Court?' She smiles.

'No. I just meant, are there any more procedures to go through?'

Marce, for once, seems disconcerted. Evidently he's been more anxious about the hearings than he's let on.

'We would like to thank you both for your conduct as EuDeFor officers,' says the chair, 'which as far as we can ascertain was exemplary in the most trying circumstances. This has been attested to by other witnesses and will be recorded in our final report. And your help to this inquiry has been invaluable.' She turns to an official. 'See to it that a helicopter is laid on to take these gentlemen to Hamburg in time for their flight to Madrid.'

I manage to murmur, 'Thank you, Admiral.'

She nods. 'Captain. Lieutenant.' She rises, followed by the other members of the august panel. We rise too. As they file out, Marce and I turn spontaneously to each other and embrace, back slaps and all. Are those tears in my friend's eyes? Van Raalte, hands folded in front of him, watches us, nods in approval.

'Drink?' murmurs Marce.

'Or two,' I say. 'We could even invite our lawyer, no?'

'Easy, now,' says Marce. 'Let's not go overboard.'

Our broad grins are signals of our profound relief: our naval careers are not yet over.

34.

Marce and I descend the steps of the aeroplane that's just landed at Madrid-Barajas airport. We're surprised to see snow on the tops of the low ochre hills, and piles of swept snow on the edges of the runway. As we walk into the terminal from the airport bus, fat snowflakes are descending again, flurried by the wind.

The Odyssey is nearing its end. Though I've no good reason to suspect her, it does still nag at me that, during the short weeks of my absence from our Chamberí home, my own Penelope may have finally given in to her suitors. In my mind I hear her saying, 'Why do you need to know, *cariño*? I didn't ask you when you came round to the flat stinking of sex.'

Is that enough? Maybe. But into my mind comes the absurd, entirely fantastical image of Marce's cousin Carlos scurrying away from the entrance to our block of flats in Chamberí. What is Carlos doing there, in my overanxious imagination? Payback for

Laura? And why Carlos? Why not some handsome book publisher or writer? Is Carlos the furtive lover making his escape, or an insolent suitor despatched with a flea in his ear? It would be the latter, surely? But maybe not. Opposites attract, and Carlos stands out for his brazen vulgarity... *Stop! Just stop!* I tell myself irritably.

Why do I always imagine the worst when it comes to Margalit? Am I loading onto her the guilt and shame I feel for the Laura incident? I try to push the thoughts away, and to instead visualise my wife in the good old days, her dark eyes startlingly immodest when she was caught by desire.

'Wake up,' Marce says, nudging me with his elbow. 'You're twitching in your sleep. We'll treat ourselves to an Uber to Delicias.'

The Uber's heading into Madrid when my phone rings. It's the palliative care nurse, Mari-Carmen, in charge of my mother's treatment at home. She tells me Elena is deteriorating and that it won't be long.

Marce tells the driver to go via Elena's flat.

I've thought a lot about Elena while I've been away in Kiel, and I regret I didn't spend more time with her while she was well. That we didn't have all the conversations we could have had about her past and her identity. About that strange and weighty idea of *Sefarad*, lost and found, and what it meant to her as a Spanish Jew. It would have helped me understand Margalit better, I think, and myself too.

The Uber drops me at my mother's flat and goes on its way south. The nurse opens the door to me. In the couple of weeks since I last saw her, the change in Elena's appearance is shocking. Her face is a yellowish mask. Like parchment. A drip is in her emaciated arm.

The nurse fusses around her, kind in a professional way. 'She's not in pain any more.'

'She was in pain?'

'It took a while to sort out. There's almost always pain at this stage.'

I sit at the bedside, and take hold of Elena's fingers.

'Is that you, *cariño*? Pass me the cup with water, my mouth is dry.' She talks with almost still lips, like a ventriloquist. 'How are you?'

'I'm fine, *mamá*. And you, how's it going?'

'As you see, could be better. But I have my morphine pump.' She coughs and puts her fist to her mouth. 'And Margalit?'

'I'm only just back from Germany, so I haven't seen her since—'

'David.' She rubs my hand. 'Please. Humour me. I'm dying, after all.' She tries to laugh, but it sounds fake, as if saying the words has brought her imminent death into sudden focus.

'I plan to,' I say, 'it's my top priority.' I bend forward to kiss her forehead.

'So it should be,' she says, and it sounds like a statement of moral certainty. Very black and white.

She closes her eyes. Her breath is shallow and quick. The room begins to close in on me. The smells of medication, antiseptic wipes, stuffy air – Elena cannot now bear the slightest draught – are oppressive. My mother is dying, and I know I've not made the most of her in my life. At worst, I've neglected her. Do I have to lose her to realise what she means to me? Without warning, the black cloud starts to descend. Elena's breathing comes in rasps. As if intuiting my thoughts, she murmurs, hardly audible through her cracked lips. 'Give me a moment, David, *cariño*.'

'I don't want to—'

'Please. Give me a moment, Mari-Carmen is here if I need anything.'

I get up, pace the room, tempted to throw open the window and breathe the fresh air.

She begins to cough, and Mari-Carmen appears. 'Your mother has to have her medication, and her bed linen needs changing,' she says.

'I'll grab myself a coffee in the street,' I mutter.

'That's fine.'

I go down and find a bar, order a café solo. I try not to think of Mari-Carmen cleaning up my mother, changing her, giving her pills and injections, adjusting her morphine drip. I glance at the news headlines on my phone. But it's all so distant and abstract, I feel like I'm in a tight knot of personal concerns, that nothing real exists beyond them.

I drink my coffee quickly and walk back to the apartment building, take the lift to Elena's flat. The nurse answers the door, her hands held strangely by her side.

'I'm sorry, Captain,' she says, and leads me into the bedroom. My mother lies with a sheet up to her chin, the angles of her cheekbones pushing at her thin skin, her hair brittle, her hands on the coverlet twisted and aged. The nurse says, 'Sometimes, you know, they'll wait until they've seen the people they want to see, and then they'll go, without fuss. I just nipped to the kitchen to make a sandwich and when I came back... Anyway, she was very peaceful just before she passed away, I'm sure it's because you've come that she felt she could let go. I'll leave you with her, I'll be in the kitchen.'

She hands me an envelope. 'Señora Pereyra has left you this, about the arrangements.'

I sit at the bedside and stroke the hand, which is still warm, and bend over and kiss the cheek. It's taut, like it's been stretched. I feel alone.

I take a taxi to Marce's flat. He sees my grim expression and folds me in an embrace. 'You all right, *hermano*?'

I manage to mutter an answer. 'She died.'

'I'm sorry, David.'

'I'm okay,' I say. 'Pleased I saw her. I have a pile of things to do.'

I start by making a call to the *Hebrá Kadishá*, the Holy Society of the Jewish Community of Madrid.

'I'm at a loss,' I say, and as I say it, I feel utterly bereft.

'That's what we're here for, friend,' says the man at the other end of the line.

The words, corny yet consoling, hinting that I'm not alone, bring a catch to my throat. I just murmur to let him know I'm still there. He explains how, when the time comes, women members of the society will ritually wash the body of Elena, and dress her in a white garment made of seven pieces of linen stitched together, without pockets, and they'll place earth under her head and shards of pots on her eyes, and settle her in her plain pine coffin, and the Society will convey the coffin to the cemetery at the appointed time – tomorrow or the day after – and men from the Society will act as pallbearers to take the coffin to the graveside. The Holy Society will send mourners, brief a rabbi who'll conduct the service, and guide me through my role in it all.

As the voice at the end of the phone goes on, explaining to me the process with gentle calm, I begin to shiver and cannot stop. I've faced enemy fire, for Christ's sake; I'm a commander of men.

But I feel the grandeur of the moment: the everyday passage from life to death of a loved one. I have a part to play that I cannot shirk. At the graveside, with the help of the other mourners, I'll perform *k'riá*, the rending of my garments, near the heart. 'It is part of grieving,' says the voice on the phone, 'it gives expression to grief and anger, which is always there. It is...' and the voice hesitates, as if searching for a secular term, '... cathartic.'

Later, I find the sheets of paper which Margalit gave me, with the transliterated words of the mourner's *kaddish*, and I read them aloud several times, nervous at the thought of public performance. I feel the need for Margalit's comforting arms around me, but there's little chance of that. She'll have heard that Elena has died; she was on the nurse's list of people to call. I wonder if she'll be at the funeral.

35.

One of the members of the *Hebrá Kadishá*, a sympathetic, heavily bearded young guy, late twenties, has met me at Elena's flat, and he gives me a lift to the Jewish cemetery in Hoyo de Manzanares. On the way, we talk about Elena, and our jobs in 'normal' life. He's a software engineer, he tells me. I stutter something about only learning I was Jewish as an adult. He says it makes no difference. A Jew is a Jew. I don't say that that, for me, is the problem. I tell him the community treated Elena pretty badly. He says, things are changing, slowly, but they are changing. For example, some communities, even in Spain, have accepted gay marriage, despite what it says in the Bible about 'a man lying with a man'. I think of Arturo and his Julián.

We arrive at the cemetery on the outskirts of the town. High walls of light-grey stone blocks, anti-Semitic graffiti. *Raus Juden, Holocuento*, and so on. The antisemites are multilingual, it seems. The path to the chapel is lined with cypresses and is calming.

The rabbi greets me, asks me about Elena and her life, and introduces the other members of the Holy Society who'll act as pallbearers.

'When do I recite the *kaddish*?' I ask. I fiddle with the knot of my dark tie and wriggle my shoulders, uncomfortable in my charcoal grey suit and over-coat. I adjust my trilby, a present from Margalit. The wintry sunshine is a big contrast with the snow of a couple of days earlier.

'*Tranquilo.* We'll let you know when the moment comes,' says one of the pallbearers.

A handful of elderly women arrive. They turn out to be aunts or distant cousins of Elena's, and they greet me with limp hands and averted eyes, as if Elena's sins of youth have still not been repaid in their moral book-keeping. The sins of the parents, and all that. One of the few biblical verses I recall. What a vengeful mind, making children pay for what their forebears have done.

Another woman comes up to me, in her seventies or older. She holds my arm and talks to me as if we've been friends for years. She seems to know a lot about me and the circumstances of my birth and adoption, and she's sarcastic about the other members of the family. It turns out she's the younger sister of Elena's father. My great-aunt Raquel. She quarrelled with her family over their treatment of her niece, and chose exile rather than to stay. For more than forty years she's lived in Barcelona and is a member of one of the newer Jewish congregations, dominated by descendants of Ashkenazi refugees from central Europe and the inevitable Argentinians. 'The old guard will have to change,' she says.

The rabbi cuts the pocket of my shirt with a pair of scissors, and a mourner approaches and rips the tear until the loose fabric rolls forward. I feel like a soldier being stripped of his medals and rank. But as the service wears on, the torn pocket is more a proud badge, a sign of continuity with my past.

'Blessed is the Lord our God, the Judge of Truth,' intones the rabbi.

As the coffin is lowered into the grave, the mourners begin to sing a psalm, and the rabbi translates a few lines into Spanish.

Surely he shall deliver thee
from the hunter's snare
and from the pernicious pestilence.
... beneath his wings shalt thou find refuge;
his truth shall be thy shield and rampart.
Thou shalt not fear the terror that stalks by night,
nor the arrow that flieth by day...

There's a heavy silence that seems to make the air vibrate. Then the rabbi talks of Elena. His brief eulogy manages to be humorous and affectionate, stitching together random details into a small, warm tribute. 'And,' he concludes, 'the *neshama*, the soul, has left the body of Elena Pereyra Rozas and with all her memories, experiences and beliefs, her sins and her good deeds, it is making its way to the Eternal World. But a part of it will have touched her son, David, and may this grant him comfort and relief. Like all before her and all who come after her, Elena is buried in a simple white shroud, so that all, rich and poor, are alike in death and equal before God.'

The faithful departed, I think, and find myself murmuring, 'Amen.'

Now one of the members of the Holy Society nods and I come forward as I've been coached, and bend down and take a handful of the pale yellow earth, and throw it into the grave. It makes a spattering sound. For once, I feel the weightiness of my elusive Jewishness, of having come from somewhere, of possessing a place in the story.

The rabbi makes a small sign with his hand. I take the sheets of paper from my pocket and recite the mourner's *kaddish*. It has a solemnness to it, a gravity, like the sound of an organ in mass. *Yisgadal, v'yiskadash, sh'meh rabá*. The men and women of the Society join with me in the prayer, and at intervals call *Amen*, and when once or twice I stumble, their voices buoy me up and help me through.

After a final *Amen*, I feel dazed, disembodied. There are whispered words of encouragement. I make my way through the two brief lines of mourners. Each person takes my hand in theirs, murmurs some consoling phrase and lets me move on. The rabbi at the head says something in Hebrew, and then, 'May God comfort you among all the mourners of Zion and Jerusalem.'

An arm is thrust through my arm and I look, and it's Margalit, and behind her a boy, on the verge of puberty. My son, Rubencito, Rubén! The lad puts out his hand and rubs my back, in an almost fatherly way. My heart lifts and tears come, despite myself. I smile through them.

'I thought you wouldn't make it.'

'We snuck in at the back,' Margalit says. 'Did you come by car?'

'Yes, one of the *Hebrá* people gave me a lift.'

'I'll give you a lift back.'

'It's okay, you don't have to.'

'I'd like to.'

Rubén is clinging to my other arm, looking up at me, pale, red-eyed and silent, but smiling.

'Are you at Marce's?' Margalit asks.

'Yes. We've just got back from Kiel.'

'Of course. How did it go?'

'We're waiting for the official report, but we've been told informally that we won't be criticised. Though EuDeFor will get it in the neck. Deservedly.'

'Fantastic. I'm so glad for you. It must be a relief.'

'Yes.' I can see it's a relief for her too. 'And I'm to be commended, apparently, for my leadership.'

Rubén gives me little play punches in the arm, a sign of his delight.

'I'll tell you more another time. Are you coming back to Elena's place? The Holy Society have organised refreshments.'

'I'd love to come. I have to drop Rubén back at school on the way.'

'Where's Sara?' I ask.

'At school. She has tests.'

'Really?'

'It's not her family.'

'No.'

'Loved the book, though.'

'What book?'

'The book you gave her for Hanukkah. Super-sophisticated, is what she said.'

'Really? Not unsuitable or anything?'

'She's pleased with the Zara gift voucher, too. So, don't worry, you're in her good books.'

'Better books.'

After we've left Rubén at the school gates, I say, 'How's he doing? I mean, with me not there.'

'Could be better. He was very upset about Elena, obviously.' She sighs. 'It'd be great if you could sit down and tell him the rest of the story. He was so delighted when you told him about the zip ties. Hasn't stopped going on about it. He'd love to know more. As I said before, you don't have to tell him every gory detail.'

'Do you want to know the gory details?'

'Not so much. But I do want to talk. About what you've been through, yes, and I also want you to understand, really understand, what it's been like for me. I need you to hear me.'

'Yes, I get that.'

After a pause, she says, 'Great that you've done the right thing by Elena. Seeing you there at the cemetery, saying *kaddish*, was…'

'What?'

'I don't know. I felt, like, this man's part of my world, you know? Not just in his own personal insulated… box. Sorry, I'm not expressing myself very well.'

'Not "self-hating"?'

'No, I mean… Self-avoiding, maybe. I don't know. Anyhow, it helps a lot.'

A handful of aunts and mourners have come back to Elena's flat and eat the snacks and drink glasses of white wine. The woman from Barcelona, Raquel, exchanges addresses, and promises to keep in touch. 'I'm family, after all!'

And finally we're alone in the living room. The air's heavy with Elena's recent presence, but also bereft of her as if she's never been.

'Come back to our place,' Margalit says. 'We could talk, it would be more comfortable there.'

36.

Rubén sits on the sofa beside me. He's very pale. He wants to snuggle up to me, a cushion clutched to his chest. Don Rafael would never have consented to that. I have to admit, it's comforting, the trust it implies, and the warmth of his body against mine. He's at that point when one moment he's a savvy almost-teenager, the next he's just a kid again, young for his age. The old woman opposite is on her balcony, but she's not interested in us, she's focusing on her potted plants. I'm almost pleased to see her.

I've asked Rubén about school and about his friends, and he's given me his usual laconic answers. He'd prefer to talk about my 'adventures'. Fair enough. It might help us reconnect, father and son. And if I can do that, maybe Margalit will be more receptive when she and I get to have our own discussions.

I've told him about the sinking, about how I moved up the Curonian Spit. I omitted my infected leg, Kamilè.

'What happened to the other people from your ship?'

'I don't know. We got separated. Some got caught. They could be in a prison or somewhere. Or... I don't know.'

'Dead?'

'Could be. But it was so good to meet up with Marce on the ferry, I didn't know if I'd see him again.'

Rubén likes Marce, he thinks he's cool. 'A lot of fighting?' he asks.

'We didn't see much,' I say. 'But we heard some shooting and rockets going off. Big booms and the ground shaking.'

'Scary.'

'Yes, scary when it's close. Loads of bombed and burnt-out buildings and craters.'

'And dead bodies?'

I wonder if he's imagining it like scenes from one of his video games. 'A few. Not like hundreds or anything.'

'Dozens?'

'A few.'

I tell him how we ate whatever we could find or steal or dig up.

'Were you hungry?'

'Very. All the time. Raw spuds for tea, imagine. If you were lucky!'

Rubén grins.

'And we had to break up furniture in buildings and burn it to keep warm. Marce knows how to do these things.'

'Proper boy scout, is Marce.'

I chuckle. 'He certainly is.'

'Why didn't EuDeFor come and rescue you?'

'They tried, after we'd met up with a group of stranded EuDeFor soldiers at one point, but it was too dangerous. The militias shot down the rescue helicopter and EuDeFor couldn't afford to send another. They're incredibly expensive.'

'How much?'

'I don't know, twenty-five million maybe.'

'Euros?'

'Yes.'

'Twenty-five million up in flames. What a waste of money.' He takes hold of my hand and plays with my fingers. His are slender and smooth, like his mother's.

'Did you have to kill anyone?'

'Hmm. Don't think so.'

'I'm going to do self-defence. *Krav M'gá*. There's going to be special classes at the synagogue.'

'Good idea.'

He says, 'So? How did you get away? From the Warriors, I mean, after they captured you.'

'We were packed on these trucks with other prisoners, driving up a steep wooded hillside, with a big slope down to one side. Then I give the signal—'

'Which was?'

'I winked. Like this.'

Rubén laughs. 'Sure. And then?'

'We break our ties, like I showed you, jump over the side of the truck, which is going slowly because it's uphill and a winding road, and throw ourselves down the slope into the gully.'

'Didn't you hurt yourselves?'

'Irbe got a bit bruised. He was our interpreter.'

'What do you mean, your *interpreter*?'

'We couldn't speak the language, so we brought him along. He spoke about six languages, he could tell us what was going on.'

'Fair enough. You paid him, I hope.'

'No, but we saved his life a few times. So anyway, all hell breaks loose, with other prisoners trying to escape, and a load of shooting. We hid in the woods until the shooting stopped and the trucks drove off. Got some boots and food off the dead militiamen. And I found my mobile which they'd got, and—'

'What about the other prisoners? Did they make it?'

'Some of them did, I'm sure.' A little lie – most were shot in cold blood. 'Then we marched north for, I don't know, ten days, maybe. Had a few adventures.'

'Such as?'

'Like getting stuck in a bog.'

'You?'

'Yep. Got distracted, fell in. Marce and Irbe saved me.'

I tell him in jokey terms about the episode. 'So I'm up to my waist in bog water, and Irbe goes, "Lie on your back, Captain, and then it's like rowing with arms! And kicking legs, like frog."'

Rubén laughs.

'And Marce says, "Swim! You're in the blank-blank navy, aren't you," which was less helpful.'

Of course, I spare him the details of how terrified I was and how close I came to drowning, that I was distracted because my thoughts were winding back to Margalit; how, despite everything – exhaustion and hunger, the penetrating chill – I'd felt a rush of desire for her and was imagining running my hand up the inside of her thigh, our deep kisses... and I'd lost my footing.

'Scary.'

'Yes. But they fished me out and got me warm and dry. Then we got lost in the bogland. Hour after hour. All you see is bog and more bog and more bog, and sometimes a few trees. By this time Irbe can hardly walk because his boots are too tight, so I put moss on his feet.'

'Moss? Because?'

'It has antiseptic properties, and it's soothing. So if you ever get lost with sore feet on the bogland of Lithuania, or anywhere else, Rubencito, you know what to do. Also good for wiping your bum with.'

'Please!'

I say nothing, of course, about Marce and me arguing over whether to leave Kaspars behind, about our differing views of the price worth paying for survival.

'We then got attacked by a helicopter, a Russian Mi-24 according to Marce. They look like insects, one huge round eye at the front.'

'Attacked, like bombed?' Rubén pulls on my arm, as if to drag me away from danger.

'Not bombed. Shot at. With heavy machine guns. Just as some militia or other was about to capture us. With wolf dogs!'

'Wow. Wolf dogs? Like, head of a wolf, body of a chihuahua?'

He grins, pleased with himself, more so when I laugh.

'Not quite. They're special dogs the Russians have bred. Like wolves but very well trained. If their handler says, "Kill!", that's what they'll do.'

'And they were going to kill you?'

'I don't know, I guess so.'

'But weren't you terrified? I would have been.'

'Yes, I was. Because humans you can communicate with, argue with. Dogs, you can't bargain or negotiate with them, they just keep coming.'

'Like the Terminator.'

What I don't say is that I was moments away from death, lying on the ground at the militiamen's mercy. Trying to curl into a ball, being kicked in the head and kidneys. Their dogs were the *volkosoby*, wolf dogs – snarling nightmares, up on their hind legs, straining at their leashes. Their handlers could barely control them. You get this primal fear, deep in the chest and guts. The old part of the brain kicks in. *Do they go for the throat first*, you're thinking, *or the genitals?*

My pulse is racing at the memory. I take a deep breath.

'Fortunately for us,' I say, 'the helicopter shot the militias by mistake instead of us, and killed them. And the dogs as well.'

I don't bother to go into the fact that it was probably all *maskirovka*, a deception, a masquerade, a performance. You confuse your enemies and do what you have to do. In this case, making sure the right pro-Russian militias come out on top, and the others don't make it. Or perhaps it was simply one of those cock-ups that happen in armed conflicts. I'm reminded, for some reason, of Marce's monologues on 'faithfulness'. Probably because deceiving one's wife requires a level of personal maskirovka I'm not capable of. Hence my relief when Margalit made it clear she knew I'd slept with someone.

'I'm not all that keen on dogs,' Rubén is saying.

'Me neither.'

'According to Mum, it's not a very Jewish thing to have dogs. Especially because of the Nazis using them. I'll ask the *Krav M'gá* instructor what to do if a dog attacks you.'

'Good idea. Kick it in the nuts, I guess.'

He laughs. 'After they shot the dogs, what happened?'

'We thought we'd lost Irbe, the human scarecrow.'

'Why do you call him that? Bit disrespectful, no?'

'Affectionate, really. Because when we found him, he was absolutely filthy. His trousers had more holes in than trouser, and his hair was so long and tangled you could barely see his face.'

'Don't tell me – then he goes *whoosh!*, and rips his rags off and turns into an interpreter?'

'Something like that.'

'With a big 'I' on his chest in a shield, SuperInt.'

'Yeah. Anyway, Marce gave him a haircut with an army knife and he looked even more like a scarecrow.'

'I'll get Marce to cut my hair, maybe.'

'I wouldn't if I were you, it's not one of his skills.'

'So Irbe's lost?'

'It turns out we hadn't lost him at all. He was lying face-down in the mud. Scared to death, he was. After the helicopter had gone, he gets up, going, "It's a miracle!" and that he'll see his wife and kids again soon. But he'd told us back where we'd found him that they'd been killed by the militias, even showed us a photo of their bodies, supposedly.'

'So he lied?'

'Exactly. He said he had to lie to us about his family or we'd have left him behind.'

'So you shot him, or what?'

'You're joking, I hope. No, of course we didn't shoot him. There are rules, even in war.'

Rubén can't get his head around the idea that you can kill each other but only subject to rules. But then again, he watches cage fighting on TV, so why would he expect rules of war?

'Marce wanted to leave Irbe out on the bog,' I continue, 'but I said that he knew the territory and spoke Latvian so he'd come in handy. So we let him come with us. And that decision probably saved our lives.'

'So if he hadn't been any use, you would've shot him?'

'Ha-ha!'

'You make it across the bog. Then what?'

'It's a long story, and I've got to get back home.'

I get up from the sofa and he says, 'All that really happened to you?'

'Yes, it really happened.'

'So you're a hero in a way, Dad?'

'No, there aren't any heroes in that kind of story. Just people trying to stay alive.'

'Well, you stayed alive.'

'We did.'

'I want to hear the ending.'

'The ending is I got back in one piece!'

'No, I mean...'

'I'll tell you another time, the final episode, in full. I promise.'

He looks at me, too solemn for an eleven-year-old. 'Isn't *this* your home?'

'How d'you mean?'

'You said you had to get back home.'

'I meant, back to Marce's...'

'Can't you stay here?'

I put my hand on his shoulder. 'Things are a bit tricky at the moment, *hijo mío*.'

'I don't like it, *papi*, you not being here.' He's holding back tears.

I kiss his head. 'I know. We're trying to sort it.'

'Yeah. Mum said. There must be a way. It can't be that difficult.'

37.

I'm back round at the Chamberí flat this afternoon. Margalit hands me post that has arrived. It includes a card from Rocío. A rather old-fashioned condolences card that reads *May God grant you strength to cope with this loss*, with a photo of a bunch of white carnations on the front and a message inside in Rocío's neat, slightly backward-sloping handwriting: *I am thinking of you, David, at this difficult time, all my love, mamá*, and after that, in careful printed letters, *Rocío Beltrán de Aguilera*. A delicate touch, I think, to spell out which *mamá* it is.

'Sweet of her,' says Margalit. 'You should get in touch, she'll want to know how you're doing.'

'Yes, I must.'

We talk about Elena and the funeral. She says, 'I want you to do the same for me if I die before you. Because I'm going to do the same for you if it falls to me.'

I ask about Rubén, and about Sara, her friends, her progress at school.

'You know Rubén's preparing for his bar mitzvah?'

'So soon?'

'He's turning twelve. Not too early to start learning his portion.'

'He mainly sends me screenshots showing his scores in video games, which I have to pretend to be interested in. But he hasn't mentioned anything about his bar mitzvah.'

'I hope you'll be there.'

I look at my wife, talking about our son's bar mitzvah. Her face may have become more lined over the past months, certainly more than before I set off for the Baltics, but the triangular shape is beautiful, her eyes dark and as calmly disconcerting as always, her lips still so kissable.

The words are out of my mouth before I know it. 'Have you been seeing anyone? I mean, since I moved out.'

'Why are you even asking?'

'If we can't be honest with each other, how do we build – rebuild – trust? And because I'm scared you have been. Seeing someone.'

'Being honest isn't always a question of what you do, David, it's about your feelings towards the other person.'

She's looking me in the eye, her head forward and slightly lowered. That old, disarming intimacy in her gaze. It's been a long, long time since she's looked at me like that.

'I know you had sex with Feigenbaum's ex-wife. I care, of course I care. But it's not the end of the world.'

'I'm sorry,' I mutter, 'I was drunk and angry…'

'It doesn't matter now.'

I'm caught by surprise. I was gearing myself up for a difficult conversation on the subject of my unfaithfulness. Perhaps it's because she herself was unfaithful to Arturo. *He who is without sin*, and all that.

She says, 'I don't want to talk about it. I've turned the page. I want you to as well.'

That's her challenge to me. The price she's exacting, or the penance she's imposing: that I move on. That I don't wallow in my Catholic guilt and shame, the luxury of self-reproach. Not the reaction I was expecting from her. It's unnerving still to be surprised after all these years by the woman you love; invigorating, too.

'I'd still like to know if you've been seeing anyone,' I say.

'And if I said yes? What then?'

'I don't know, I don't know.' I rub my hands up and down over my eyes.

She moves next to me on the sofa and puts her arm around me. 'I didn't sleep with anyone else, okay. Satisfied?'

I feel wretched.

'Even though I had the opportunity. Opportunities, plural. But I didn't have the motive. So I didn't.'

'Who did you not sleep with?'

'David, stop it. And you go on about trust. I'm telling you I'm not interested in other men.'

'I'm sorry, I'm sorry.' I slump forward, my hands between my knees, looking at the floor, feeling guilty.

We sit for a while in silence.

'She was a brave woman, your mother. I had a lot of time for her. How are you coping, really?'

'I don't know, I'm still processing it. I've become terribly… fond of her.' Again a silence. I take a breath and turn to look at her. 'Margalit, darling, I know I've not… but is there any hope, any possibility we might actually sort something out, come to some kind of accommodation?'

'*Accommodation*?' Her tone is gently mocking.

'You're answering a question with a question!'

'Yep. That's what being Jewish is about. Provisionality. Loose ends. Accommodation. Hmm, yes, It's a possibility. Rubén certainly expects it of us.'

'My feelings haven't changed,' I murmur.

'Nor have mine, *tonto*.'

She kisses me, lips soft, like in the old days, and I feel the blood pulsing at my throat.

'Can I stay?' I ask. I'm sure I have the forlorn look of a little boy.

She strokes my face. 'I don't think that's a good

idea. Not yet. But Rubén's dying to hear about the rest of your *adventure*.'

'Okay. Maybe you'll sit with us?'

'I'll think about it. But I wouldn't want to cramp your style, and anyway, "thrillers" aren't my cup of tea.'

'I thought you loved it when your grandad Isaac told you about his adventures with the Greek partisans?'

'Ah, that was then. And I wasn't worried sick about him the way I have been about you, *cariño*.'

She kisses my cheek and goes through to the kitchen to prepare the evening meal for her and the kids, leaving me in a state of bewildered, exhilarated arousal.

38.

A few days later, Rubén sends me a WhatsApp message, *Next episode!*, and an emoji of a gun which on closer inspection turns out to be a water pistol. I message him, *After school this evening?*

He's waiting in the living room. He shouts, 'Mum!', and Margalit calls back, 'Coming.'

'She's asked to sit in,' he says, 'and I thought that was reasonable.'

'But I don't think she wants to listen to my so-called exploits, Rubencito. I asked her before.'

'She is right here, you know,' says Margalit.

She sits down in an armchair. 'Don't mind me.'

Of course, that makes me feel I'm under observation, subjected to some test, like a driving test, whose rules and purpose I don't understand and whose pass mark is unknown.

'Okay, Dad,' he says, 'so last time, you and Marce and the human scarecrow had escaped the horrible dogs and were heading for his hometown, right?'

I glance at Margalit, but she has her inscrutable face on.

'Right,' I say, 'we shouldn't call him the scarecrow.'

'You literally did!'

'I know, I know, but Kaspars Irbe is his name. Kaspars, okay, satisfied?'

Rubén giggles. Is that the faintest of smiles on Margalit's lips?

'So anyway, we come into Grobiņa – Kaspars's town – at dusk. He's leading the way. We go through streets with little whitewashed houses. They've all got gardens and fruit trees and a few chickens, and you can see fields and open country through the gaps between them.'

'So it's practically the countryside still?'

'Exactly. Then Kaspars stops outside one of the houses.'

'Chickens?'

'Yes. And some big white geese. He goes up to the front door and rings the bell. A large woman with red cheeks comes out and stands there with her arms folded. Suspicious expression.'

'Why suspicious?'

'Because she doesn't recognise him. He's a human scarecrow, don't forget.'

Rubén laughs. 'Dad! Don't call him that. You made a rule and you broke it. That's not setting a good example.'

'Sorry.' I glance again at Margalit, expecting some wry twitch of the mouth, a response to the idea of my rule-breaking. But she's impassive, avoiding eye contact, very still as if trying to meld with the furniture.

'She doesn't recognise Kaspars,' I continue. 'He's limping and filthy and wearing rags. She gets this amazed expression, like she's seen a ghost, and she goes, "Irbe?" in a whisper.'

'And then?'

'She goes purple, and she slaps him really hard.'

'What! Why?'

'Because she's so angry at him for disappearing and she was so scared he was dead.' I daren't look at Margalit. 'The woman starts screaming and Kaspars turns to Marce and translates. "She said, What happened to your fucking hair, Irbe! And your fucking teeth! You look like an imbecile." Marce and I start roaring with laughter and—'

'Dad! Language!'

'Sorry, Rubencito, you're right. But that's what she said and I'm trying to be accurate.'

'Okay, fair enough when it's just the two of us, but not in front of Mum.'

'Point taken.'

Out of the corner of my eye I see Margalit trying hard not to grin, her mouth wobbling. I relax a bit.

'So Kaspars is absolutely delighted with himself. Delighted that she's shouting at him. She grabs him, and squeezes his skinny body in her meaty arms and kisses him all over his face, like he's an ice lolly.'

'A human ice lolly. Yuck.'

'A human scarecrow ice lolly, in fact.'

'Dad!' He mock-punches me. I make a move, as if I'm about to tickle him.

He lets out a yelp of laughter. 'No! Stop. That's child cruelty!'

'Fair point. So anyway, the woman, she's very annoyed we're laughing, but Kaspars explains we saved his life. More than once. Then two shy, pretty little blonde-haired girls turn up and hide behind her skirts. Kaspars sees them and escapes his wife and scoops them up and kisses them. Sofi and Emi. That was Kaspars's family, and they let Marce and me stay for a couple of days and rest a bit, and they fattened us up with good food. I tell you, Rubencito, the smell of pork sausages and cabbage that first night was the most delicious thing I've ever smelt in my life.'

'Pork? You ate pork?'

I can sense Margalit's gaze on me, waiting for my answer. 'Well it probably wasn't pork,' I say lamely. 'It was probably veal or something.'

'Come on, Dad, you can't expect me to believe that. You promised no bullshit.'

'Okay, you're right, it was pork.'

Rubén breathes out dramatically, shaking his head in mock reproof. I try to forget that Margalit is still sitting there. If it had just been her and me, my account would have been different, less flamboyant and risky, less jokey. But Rubén has changed the dynamic, brought forth this version of events. Is that a good thing? I don't know.

'But it's allowed,' I say, 'when you're literally starving, which we were.'

Rubén makes a face and nods slowly, suggesting that he's reluctantly letting me off the hook. 'Okay,' he says.

'And the next day, she killed a goose. And that's definitely kosher.'

He frowns. 'So you're in a safe town, right, where Kaspars lives?'

'Grobiņa. Not exactly safe. You can hear rockets a few kilometres away, and explosions, and at night it's all lit up. So no one feels really safe.' I wonder as I'm speaking what's happened to Kaspars and his family. I haven't heard from him since we got home, hope he's all right.

'Grobiņa's still a fair distance from the sea,' I continue, 'which means we had to work out a way of getting to another town, called Liepaja, I think that's how you say it, which is a port where you can get a boat to Germany.'

'Why didn't you phone home, Dad?'

'I couldn't.'

'Why not?'

I'm aware again of Margalit's presence. Of the fact that I'm addressing her as well as my son. 'I couldn't because the lines were down, and there was no mobile signal, and my phone was...'

I hesitate, because the real reason is that I knew it was dangerous and we still might not make it. That would have been far worse for Rubencito, and for Margalit, to raise their hopes then dash them. She'd have heard reports of the Pandora's sinking and might have already given up hope of seeing me again. Weeks had passed since then. I barely knew what date it was. How would she react? How long do you have to wait before a person can be declared missing, presumed dead? What happens, in Jewish ritual, when there's no body to bury?

'Dad? You were saying?'

'I wanted to send a telepathic message to you and your mum saying, "I'm alive! I'm alive! Don't give up on me! I'm trying to come home!" But of course I couldn't.'

'I never thought you were dead.' Rubén rubs my hand. 'Don't stop now. How did you get to the port?'

'Yes, so Kaspars agrees to be our guide as far as Liepaja. Monika, Kaspars's wife, gives us packets of food and hugs us. It's like being in a bear hug, it's a wonder he's survived the marriage.'

Rubén laughs.

'She says something to Kaspars. He grins – he's lost most of his bottom teeth—'

'Which helps with the scarecrow vibe.'

'Exactly.'

Rubén and I smirk at each other, complicit in the silly joke.

'Carry on.'

'And Kaspars goes, "She says you better send me back to her alive! If I'm not alive, she says to me, don't bother coming back!"'

'Mum's not like that.'

'Everybody's different, Rubén.'

I turn to Margalit, and she's getting up, without a word but with a definite half-smile, and she heads off in the direction of the kitchen.

39.

Rubén and I stay chatting and laughing on the sofa for a while. I ask him about his schoolwork but he'd rather talk about what level of *Call of Duty* he's reached. 'It wouldn't be for you, Father, you're practically an old person and your reflexes are too slow.' He easily dodges my pretend swipe. Margalit comes back into the living room. She puts on that look of hers that means, *What are they up to now, the pair of them?*

Have I passed the test? Who knows.

'Rubén, haven't you got homework to do?' says his mum.

'I want to carry on with Dad's story.'

'Go on,' I say, 'off you go. We'll finish it another time. You know how it ends.'

'Yes,' he says, 'but it's the *journey* that counts, isn't it, *papi*.' He grins, knowing he's scored a point. 'Ma, can I go round to Daniel's to do my homework? We're working on the same project.'

'Yes. But be back by eight for dinner.'

'I might eat something there.'

'Ring me if you do.'

'Sure. Oh, and Dad...'

'Yes?'

He takes me by the arm and leads me to the hallway. 'I'm a bit nervous about my bar mitzvah.'

'It's not for months, is it?'

'No, but I'm scared about standing up in front of all those people and singing my portion of the Torah and the Haftorah.'

'It's not really singing, from what I understand. More chanting.'

'No, Dad, there are proper notes. I've got a bit where Shadrach, Mishach and Abednego get thrown into Nebuchadnezzar's fiery furnace. But they survive.'

'Fiery furnace, I don't think I remember that bit. I'm probably not the right person to ask about bar mitzvahs – have you spoken to Simón? But you can go through it with me if you like. Maybe tomorrow. I'll be the congregation.'

'Thanks, Dad.'

He grabs his school bag and runs off.

'Have you got any money on you?' calls his mother, but he's already out of the front door. I go back to the living room and sit on the sofa.

'I'm so pleased you're telling him about your adventures. It's wonderful for him, helps him understand what you've been through, and feel you're not just an absent father. But I'd love to know what you're missing out.'

'The best bits,' I say.

She frowns at my facetiousness. 'So how are you doing, really?'

'Okay. I'm fine. Fine. Well, not so fine, actually. The inquiry was helpful because I had to talk things through, face them. And it's great to be able to sit with Rubén and feel him opening up a bit. He's blossoming in fact, you've done a good job. But I still feel terrible about my crew.' Still struggling under that tonne-weight of guilt. Which is a good Jewish emotion, I guess. Though also very Catholic...

She's sitting close enough for me to catch the smell of her. She says, 'Last time we spoke you said you didn't like living away from us.'

'Yes.'

'So what do you propose we do about it?'

'Talk.'

'Talk?'

'Yes, it's a start, isn't it? We have a lot to sort out.' She smiles.

'You are very handsome with your weather-beaten face, you know.'

'Handsome?'

'Yes. Stop repeating what I've just said to you. And your beard, it suits you very well. You had a beard when I first met you. At that party. It was a bit darker and fuller then.'

She's looking at me in a strange way. Not strange, more like a challenge or an invitation. More like in the old days. I've been following the wrong script.

I smile. 'Okay. So I'm a real stereotype sailor now.'

'Or Lope de Aguirre, maybe.'

'Great – a crazy obsessive.'

'*Conquistador.*' She's edging very close. She says, 'Where's your mouth in all that beard? I'm guessing it's in there somewhere,' and she reaches towards me and kisses me.

After a few seconds she pulls away.

'There are more urgent things to do than talk, *cariño.*'

My guilt is a gloomy presence, and our lovemaking is tentative at first. But it doesn't matter, because afterwards we can lie in each other's arms, and I can breathe, breathe. I feel a huge sense of release, like finding an oasis in the desert. Can't remember when we'd last had sex – before the Baltics, certainly.

Later, we do talk.

'I've thought a lot about our conversation after Elena's funeral,' she says.

'Me too.'

'Something seemed to be shifting.'

'Maybe.'

I lie quietly, staring into space, flicking my gaze.

'What are you thinking?' she asks.

'Oh, nothing.'

'Look, *cariño*, don't think you have to become religious and observant, or whatever. Just meet me halfway, you know?'

'I must be nearly there, no?'

'Nearly where?'

'Halfway!'

'Give me a kiss, *tonto*!'

I raise myself on one elbow and stroke her hair. I feel an incredible lightness in my chest. I lie back and she leans over me, her hair tickling my face. 'Time to get up, lazybones.'

I say, 'So... would it be all right if I move back in? I mean, it doesn't have to be immediately, but...'

She pauses. 'I don't know, David. Maybe we had better take it slowly.'

'I know how I feel.'

She rubs my shoulder. 'Look, it's been great, just being together the two of us again. But we've been through a lot, and I want to be sure. You know?'

I do know.

40.

I told Marce that Rubén wanted to hear about zip ties and helicopters and stuff.

'I said you'd do your helicopter noise impressions, show him some tricks from your Survival 101 manual.'

'*Noise impressions?*' Marce said, in mock outrage. '*Tricks?* I'm not a performing seal, David. Knowing your helicopter sounds is a vital skill in times of conflict.'

'Absolutely,' I said. 'That's a yes, then.'

So I've brought Rubén round to Marce's place. Rubén says, 'This is where you're staying, Dad? Hmm.'

Marce's showing Rubén pictures of military helicopters on his laptop and explaining you can tell them apart by the noise they make. My lad is listening intently.

'With the Mi-24s, like that one,' – Marce points to a black and white image of the sinister swamp insect – 'you hear a kind of *chip-chip-chip* low note and then the high note. Like crickets.'

'How do you make that noise?'

'Oh, it's like beatboxing. I'll show you.' He does. Rubén tries to imitate him and fails.

'Can you do it, Dad?'

'No, I don't go in for circus tricks.' I wink at Marce.

'Is that the one that attacked you and Dad?' Rubén asks.

'Exactly. Whereas with Apaches, the noise goes through you, hits your chest. Like this.' He puts his hand to his mouth and makes whirring, thumping noises.

'How do you know so much about helicopters, Marce?' I ask, putting my arm round Rubén.

'Always wanted to be a pilot, my big dream when I was a boy. Fly a Sikorsky or a Super-Puma. A Sikorsky sounds different again. Kind of *chukka-chukka-chukka.*'

'Cool!' says Rubén.

When Marce has gone to his room, Rubén and I sit at the living-room table and I finish the story for him.

'So we walk at night from Grobiņa to Liepaja. Marce and me, with Kaspars as our guide.'

'How far?'

'I don't know, couple of hours maybe – ten, twelve kilometres along the road, but we had to make a big detour so we wouldn't be spotted. Luckily there was a bit of a moon, so we could see where we were going. We teased Kaspars all the way about how alive his supposedly dead wife seemed to us. He didn't mind.

But it's better when he doesn't grin because he's got so many teeth missing.

'After about three hours we get to the shores of a long lake. On the far side, factory chimneys. That's the town we're aiming for, Liepaja. Kaspars takes us through a maze of potholed roads with cement works and engineering workshops. Outside a factory wall, we say goodbye to Kaspars, and thank him.'

I remember Irbe standing there, shifting his weight from foot to foot, hands clasped in front of him. Standing as near to attention as he could, with his hunched frame, and saluting. 'Good luck, Captain, sir. Lieutenant, sir.' We laughed, and embraced him, Spanish-style, with back-slapping. I looked him in the eye, holding him at arm's length, and felt genuine fondness, thinking, *This man has done us a real kindness, for whatever reason, at considerable personal risk. Gemilut hasidim.* He responded to our bear hugs with awkward dabs.

'I give him a final pat and a pinch of the cheek, and we watch him walk off into the night, mission accomplished, happy as a—'

'Scarecrow?'

'No! That's not a thing, as you well know.'

Rubén giggles.

'Anyway, we meet up with our contact who turns out to be the Finnish consul, and he drives us to a safe house where we stay for a couple of days and have long hot baths and cold beers, until he can arrange travel documents and tickets, and then we take a freighter to Travemünde in Germany.'

I can still feel the relief of making it to German soil, of taking my first easy breath in weeks. No longer being hunted down, brain no longer on high alert all day, every day.

'And that's it?'

'That's it. Isn't that enough for you, Rubencito?'

'That's when you phoned home? Because I know Mum thought you were dead, but I never did.'

'Yes. The first thing I did when I got to Germany was phone home, to let you know I was alive.'

The minders allowed me a brief phone call in Travemünde before placing me and Marce in purdah. 'Oh my God, oh my God, David,' she said, shocked, choked. 'You're alive? Thank God. Where are you? I thought you were dead, I heard about the boat going down. I was so horribly scared.'

'Did they interrogate you?' Rubén asks.

'Who? EuDeFor? Of course. But first they took us to the military hospital in a place called Lübeck. Because we were suffering from malnutrition due to all the raw potatoes we had to eat, and I had cracked ribs from a collision with a militiaman's rifle butt. And we both had bleeding gums and missing teeth, and athlete's foot and rower's rash in the groin and other fungal—'

'Too much information, Father!'

'I thought you wanted the details.'

'Not those details.'

'So, anyway, then we had a debriefing with a pair of EuDeFor intelligence officers.'

'What did they want to know?'

'Mainly about the troop movements we saw on the Curonian Spit, and the different militias we'd encountered and what kind of gear they had, weapons and stuff.'

'What else?'

'Ah, top secret. If I told you, I'd have to eliminate you.'

'Ha ha.'

'And then they flew us home.'

I remember when I first saw her again, Margalit, after being given up for lost. Her suffering was etched in her features. But there she was, in full colour, vibrant, not the washed-out, two-dimensional figure in the photos on my phone. It was then I knew that I was truly home, and safe. She threw her hand to her mouth in horror at how thin I was, how lined my face, how I'd aged. The grey was spreading up my sideburns towards the temples. Some of the haggardness would fade, the gauntness would fill out. But, I wondered, as I stared at myself in the bathroom mirror, would there always be the shadow behind the eyes?

Rubén intertwines his fingers with mine, and I come back to the present, to the sound of his voice. 'Dad? Okay for Marce to come to us for *Pesach* next week?'

'Sure.'

Later, I invite Marce.

'Jewish festivals aren't my thing, you know that. When is it?'

'Next Sunday night. Candle-lighting, a few prayers and blessings, lashings of food. Wine. Please, Marce, I'd appreciate it. So would Rubén.'

Marce places his hand on my shoulder. 'David, you're nervous, aren't you?'

'Of course not. What about?'

Marce gives me that look. 'You can bullshit yourself, man, you can't bullshit me. You're nervous about moving out of here and moving back in there.'

'I don't know. Maybe you're right. Things are still a bit up in the air. But it's not that. Not only that. You know, what we've been through, you and me...'

Marce nods. 'I'm your shield, aren't I?'

'Always, man, always.'

He squeezes my arm tight. 'Same here.' He has a droll expression, pained but indulgent. 'Hell, man, *Pesach*, I'll think about it.'

41. Madrid, April 2019

I'm with Margalit and the kids. The Guinsburgs came early to help with the preparations, and now Marce has turned up too.

'Oh, here's Elijah!' says Margalit, to laughter.

She asked me before in a quiet moment whether I was going to go back to sea. I said, 'I think the sea's part of who I am, darling,' and she nodded.

If I can get another commission, that is: even one in the Baltic, even for herring. What are the chances, though? EuDeFor top brass may have had enough of me. We'll see.

I've struggled hard to work out who I am, what kind of man I am. What kind of Jew. A bad Jew, obviously; an irreligious Jew, an adopted lapsed-Catholic-Jew hybrid. I'm still working on that. But absolutely a Jew. Defined by others as such, and increasingly, defiantly, by myself: a Jew and a fighter, with history, and memories. I'll go to Elena's grave, lay a small stone on it in remembrance.

'And Israel, *cariño*? Are you still thinking your future lies in Israel?' I've avoided that question up to now.

'I don't know,' Margalit says. 'Maybe you and I can imagine ways of being together here. Or there. Who knows?'

The table is laid out for the *Pesach* dinner, the *Seder*. The Guinsburgs have brought an offering of gefilte fish simmered in stock, typically Ashkenazi. Margalit and Sara have made aubergines stuffed with spiced rice, fragrant with cinnamon and cardamom and ground coriander, and there will be brisket slow-cooked in wine with prunes and apricots, and a baked apple dessert. It's a bit of a Sephardi–Ashkenazi culinary clash, but Margalit says, 'Why not? Let's be ecumenical!' There are lit candles, and the centre plate with the charred lamb shank bone, little bowls of bitter herbs, lettuce, boiled egg, and a cinnamon-flavoured sweet paste – *charoset*, Margalit calls it – of almonds and dates and sweet kosher wine. Next to the plate is the pile of three unleavened crackers, matzos, under a napkin.

The kids – Sara, Rubén, and the Guinsburgs' two – are noisy and excited. They're taking surreptitious glugs of wine, changing the words of the traditional *Pesach* songs to make silly rhymes, and giggling. Marce laughs at them, and with them, and joins in the banter. Rubén, whose voice is breaking, has a fuzz on his chin, and is quietly joyful that everyone's together again. At least for this evening. He sits next to me, nudging into my arm. Sara is feisty and chirpy, taking no prisoners, but in a jolly kind of way, meaning she's pleased to see me. She does a twirl in front of me, showing off her new top. Something in a pastel colour with wide sleeves. 'Zara,' she says. 'Mum thinks it's a bit unsuitable.' We grin at each other.

Pesach, Simón reminds the gathering, celebrates escape against the odds from slavery and captivity in Egypt, and also survival. He looks at me and raises his glass. 'To David Aguilera and Marce Feigenbaum. They escaped, and they survived!'

Alejandra says, 'I hope they're not going to wander in the wilderness for forty years,' and the grown-ups laugh.

I shake my head.

Marce raises his glass. 'And to Margalit. She's resisted, it can't have been easy, and she's come through, and now she seems prepared to bear the additional burden of having this guy around.'

'That's enough of your speechifying, Marce,' I say, mortified.

The others are laughing, but Margalit looks disconcerted. 'Don't presume too much, the pair of you.' But then she raises her glass and joins in the laughter.

'Good Jew, bad Jew, who knows,' says Alejandra. 'He's an awkward bloody Jew, that's all one can say!'

'And a good thing too, *joder*!' shouts Simón.

There's more laughter, and I grin and begin to feel at ease again. Back home. Will it work out? Time will tell. Margalit turns, puts her hand on the back of my neck. Kisses me full on the mouth. '*Chag sameach!*' she says. 'Happy *Pesach*.'

Acknowledgements

Small Wars in Madrid has had a long and laborious journey to publication, so I have accumulated many debts of gratitude. Some two decades ago, my friend John Murphy suggested that we write a film script, about the shipwreck of men of the retreating Spanish Armada off the coast of Ireland. We wrote the screenplay, *The Rags of Men*, based on contemporary sources, were awarded a Screen West Midlands grant to develop it, and sadly never got any further. Some years later I attempted to turn it into a contemporary novel. The story went through numerous iterations.

In the end, almost nothing of the original remained, beyond the idea of a Spanish sea captain and a shipwreck. The focus changed from survival of individuals against the odds in a hostile, conflict-ridden sixteenth-century Ireland, to the protagonist's struggle to come to terms with his fractured Jewish/Catholic identity in an uncertain (and slightly alternative) contemporary world. The central theme of 'men at war' became 'a man at war' – with his family and with himself – taking in Jewishness and belonging and identifying one's place in the world. I'm very grateful to John for having set me off on this long fictional journey. My gratitude is tinged with sadness: to the shock of his many friends, John died suddenly and unexpectedly in August 2023, and I'd like to dedicate the book to his memory.

Once the novel began to emerge in its present shape, many people helped me refine the story and writing. As with my other books, I'm extremely grateful to friends Miles Larmour and Alan Mahar who read and commented on several drafts, identifying both structural problems and line-by-line sloppy writing with their usual consummate skill. To them must be now added a third close reader: my nephew, Adam Ferner, himself a writer; he made detailed and acute comments on drafts, and showed a forensic ability to hack away unnecessary verbiage.

My friends and colleagues at the Tindal Street Fiction Group have, as ever, been invaluable in their comments on the chapters of *Small Wars in Madrid* that I've brought to workshop with them over the years. Some current and past members have provided feedback on entire drafts: many thanks to Gaynor Arnold and Mez Packer. I'm specifically grateful to Michael Toolan, one of the Tindal Street members, for his valuable guidance on Catholic ritual and perceptions of the world.

My friend Huub van Abel, an avid reader of English literature, read and made observations on a previous version and noted, as others had, that it was really a family drama tied up with a thriller and – he diplomatically implied – that it needed to make its mind up which it wanted to be.

My family, as always, have been very supportive, though that's their job. My wife Diana Foster has patiently listened to countless readings of draft chapters, as have my sons, Daniel and Joseph. Their feedback is always useful and they ask the right questions. My sister-in-law Celia Moss read one of the earlier drafts, as did friend Rebecca Althaus.

Finally, I'm very grateful to Louise Boland and my meticulous editor, Sarah Shaw, at Fairlight Books for helping keep the vessel afloat. Their initial reaction to the first version I submitted to them back in 2022 was, like Huub's, that this was two books in one. They suggested a more focused and shorter book charting the emotional and psychological journey of the protagonist and his extended family. This novel is the result. I'm very grateful to Louise and Sarah for (to mix my metaphors) leaving the door ajar! I'd also like to thank the other members of the Fairlight team, Greer Claybrook, Swetal Agrawal and Beccy Fish; Sam Kalda for his superb cover illustration; Gary Jukes for his careful copyediting; and Jennifer Graves for proofreading the final version.

Also in the Fairlight Moderns series